The Redacted Sherlock Holmes – Volume III

Orlando Pearson

The words spoken by the girl in the stable in "A Seasonal Tale" are based on extracts from "High Flight" by John Gillespie Magee. The author asserts no claim to the text and uses it for solely for artistic purposes.

Paperback ISBN 978-1-78705-015-0
ePub ISBN 978-1-78705-016-7
PDF ISBN 978-1-78705-017-4

Published in the UK by MX Publishing
335 Princess Park Manor, Royal Drive,
London, N11 3GX
www.mxpublishing.co.uk

For My Family

Dr Anstruther's Practice

My reader may well consider the events described under the title "The Stockbroker's Clerk" to have been concluded definitively. That story started on a Saturday morning with Holmes picking me up from my newly opened medical practice in Paddington and the narrative then switched location to Birmingham. It ended that same evening with the apprehension in London of the case's main criminal by the police, and with the apprehension of his main accomplice in Birmingham by Holmes and me posing as an accountant and a clerk.

The main events of the day had reached their end by seven o'clock, but by the time the police had been summoned and statements taken, it was nearly midnight. Our petitioner, the stockbroker's clerk Mr Hall Pycroft, had hotel accommodation in Birmingham and elected to return to it. I was anxious to return to my wife after my unexpected day-long absence and to spend the Sunday attending to the matters that inevitably arise when one has just opened a new business. Holmes also wished to return to London at the earliest opportunity and, accordingly, he and I boarded the train that trundles slowly through the night between Birmingham and London, just as Mr Pycroft had done the night before.

I was exhausted after the long and event-filled day, but perhaps due to the swift resolution of the case, Holmes seemed more alert than ever. We were the only passengers in our compartment and, while I stretched out on the seats, Holmes sat lost in thought. I could see something was still troubling him and I knew that any interjection from me would be unwelcome.

At last he too stretched out and said, “It’s no good Watson, it won’t come to me. There remains something – some observation that I made today – that I am still unable to account for.”

“Really, Holmes? You seem to me to have solved the Pycroft case as completely as can be imagined.”

“Oh, that! The case for which I have dragged you from London to Birmingham this morning was a matter of such superficiality and my role in it so modest, I was going to suggest you withhold it from publication. The only reason why you may wish to place it before the public is to advertise your services as a doctor and to demonstrate your skill in reviving a man who was seeking to hang himself – for all that you may merely have postponed his appointment with the gallows.”

I could see that Holmes had more to say and waited for him to continue. As I waited, I turned over in my head whether the matter which Holmes proposed I should advertise would help or hinder the development of my practice.

“There is some trifling matter,” went on Holmes at last, his brow still furrowed and his flow of words slow, “some small thing of which I took note, which in the helter-skelter of solving this Birmingham case I failed to investigate. But it will not now occur to me what it is."

He drew on his pipe and sat back with his eyelids drawn three-quarters of the way over his eyes. There was a silence. I forbore to interrupt my friend's concentration as he struggled to recall the matter to which he had referred.

The night train from Birmingham to London proceeds slowly and stays off the main routes to avoid arriving in London too early. This may be why it pitched and rocked far more than one might normally expect in these times of fast, comfortable and convenient rail travel. It was as the train swayed over a particularly bumpy set of points that Holmes suddenly sat upright:

"By Jove, yes! The uneven stairs!"

"The stairs! What stairs?" I asked, puzzled as to their relevance to the mystery to which we had addressed ourselves that day.

"The stairs of your house and of your neighbour's house."

I ran my practice from a house next door to another house occupied by a medical practitioner. Both practices had opened at the same time thirty years previously and that morning Holmes had deduced that I had the better of the two because the steps leading up from the street to my front-door were more worn than those of my neighbour. I waited for my friend to continue.

"You said this morning that the revenue from your practice last year amounted to little more than three hundred pounds. This must mean that your neighbour is making much less."

"My practice was in decline when I bought it, Holmes," I said a little defensively, "because my predecessor became ill. It had previously turned over far more than three hundred pounds."

"Nevertheless, from the state of the stairs, your neighbour must earn considerably less in fee income than yours."

"That may be so. What of it?" I said, slightly nettled by my friend's sudden interest in my financial affairs and those of my neighbour.

"Yet this accommodating neighbour of yours can afford to neglect his practice to the extent that he can ask you to mind it in his absence. Moreover, he actually takes more days away than you do, for when I ask you to join me in an investigation he is in your debt in terms of days worked."

I had no comment to make to this and waited for Holmes to continue.

"Does it not strike you as strange that your neighbour can afford so much time away from his work even though his takings are much lower than yours?"

"My predecessor in my practice, Farquhar, charged higher fees than Anstruther, his neighbour," I said cautiously, not wishing to answer the question. "Farquhar therefore attracted more well-to-do people whereas Anstruther drew people from the local factories, for whom a visit to the doctor represented a substantial expense."

"Yet your steps are three inches more worn down than his, so not only does he charge his patients less than your predecessor did, but he has fewer of them."

I remained silent, but Holmes persisted.

"You see my point, Watson. Either Anstruther must accept a much lower income than you, or he must have some other means of support. Moreover, you have an additional income from the royalties arising from the somewhat sensational reports you have made of two of our adventures, so his private income must be very substantial if he can afford to be away from his practice more often than you are."

"If you must know, Holmes," I said with some acerbity as I was reluctant to enter into discussions with Holmes on my financial situation, "I received a one-off payment of £25 for "A Study in Scarlet". And the magazine selling the serialisation of "The

Sign of Four" will retail at a shilling a copy, so my share, once all deductions have been made, is likely to be of most use for insertion into the Christmas pudding."

"Does Anstruther have private means?" pressed Holmes, his interest not deflected by my quip.

"Not to my knowledge, although, as you say, he spends more time away from his practice than I do from mine, which makes what you say a permissible inference," I responded cautiously. The matters that Holmes was raising were not ones I wished to discuss with him, so I again sought to divert his focus by providing additional information. "Anstruther has a passion for painting, which is why he is often away. He tells me that he favours cloudscapes and skyscapes and often goes to East Anglia to paint them. Maybe he sells them to provide himself with a second income."

"So what are the costs of your business?" Holmes persisted, as ever responding to the thoughts that were running through my head rather than to my words.

"Really, Holmes!" I replied after a slight pause as I considered whether to respond at all. "This cannot be of concern to you. Pycroft introduced you to the notorious Beddington this evening as an accountant and this has obviously got to your head. For what it is worth, I am paying down the capital on the practice and on the house, which is also my dwelling. I additionally pay a receptionist two pounds a week as a wage and pay six shillings for her into a superannuation fund. This will pay a pension calculated as a per centage of her final salary when she retires. I also have all the outgoings of a normal householder and, to maintain the premium nature of my practice, I need to make sure the house is well maintained."

"So your outgoings considerably exceed your income," commented Holmes.

As usual my friend's speed of thought process and his lack of inhibition in expressing the outcome of it quite took my breath away. He continued: "Your receptionist is costing you one hundred and eleven pounds and sixteen shillings per annum while, if you are paying off the cost of your house over twenty-five years with the related interest and meeting the running costs of the house, that will more than exhaust your three hundred pounds of income. This is before the cost of setting up your practice. Maybe I should try and arrange for you to join me on more cases. Royalties negotiated at a more remunerative rate than what you enjoy at present from your romances may be the only way of keeping your head above water."

I stayed silent.

"And your neighbour's practice must be in even worse straits. Anstruther must have a very considerable secondary source of income to enable him to remain in his profession for, although he may have paid down his initial capital outlay, his operating costs will be the same as yours. What do your patients say about him when they have seen him in your absence?"

I was far more comfortable talking about my neighbour's practice than I was about talking to Holmes about either my own finances or those of Dr Anstruther. "They say little other than that it is less modern than my newly appointed premises, but he has been running it for many years, so this is not to be wondered at. They have not complained of the treatment. We all have our own quirks in how we administer treatment. I believe in pills and potions, whereas Anstruther believes in injections as it eliminates the delays caused by medication passing through the stomach."

To forestall further questions, I considered asking Holmes whether he was now obliged to make a commercial charge for his services, now that he was bearing the full costs of the rooms at Baker Street on his own, following my marriage. Before I could do so, however, instead of persisting with his line of forensic financial questioning, he settled back in the cushions of our train compartment and commented, "Well, we have at least identified a mystery, even if we have no reason at present to seek to solve it."

Holmes's remarks on my financial affairs were far more insightful than I had realised. When I subsequently spoke to my own accountant about my finances, he confirmed my friend's adverse assessment of them, which had escaped me in the whirl of activity to set my practice up.

"I assumed you realised that you were incurring losses on your business, Dr Watson," he commented. "The fact that you had large liabilities to everyone apart from the taxman should have told you as much." When I suggested to my accountant that the losses I was incurring were something I would have expected him to tell me about, he added, "I was focusing on ensuring that you met the onerous reporting requirements of a new business rather than on informing you whether your business was profitable or not."

It was only after these exchanges that I started to focus real attention on making my friend's activities known to a wider public. My reader may recall the results in the long list of short stories which started with "A Scandal in Bohemia", published in July 1891 after I had had the most modest returns referred to above from "A Study in Scarlett" and "The Sign of Four". My stories attracted considerable attention in the national press, and Holmes's business acumen ensured that royalties were negotiated at a highly remunerative rate. The preparation for the initial publication of these stories also coincided with the climactic events in Holmes's campaign against Moriarty, which reached their apparently tragic conclusion in May 1891. Perhaps aided by the absence of Holmes, whom I believed to be at the bottom of the Reichenbach Falls, I was able to grow my practice rapidly after the events described in "The

Final Problem", so that it delivered a revenue of over six hundred pounds in 1892.

In mid-1893 my dear Mary was carried away by the influenza and I had no desire to remain in living quarters which were now not only too big for one person but also provided constant reminders of her presence. Accordingly, I moved into modest bachelor accommodation in Church Street in Kensington, but I retained my consulting room in the house, rented out the handsome living quarters, and travelled between my new lodgings and Paddington every day. By early 1894, I had a medical practice which made a handsome profit, a satisfactory level of income from the rental of the Paddington house, and the royalties from my writings. These three sources of income comfortably offset the costs of my Kensington lodgings. Thus I could enjoy a level of pecuniary security I had never previously experienced, although, I need hardly add, my improved financial situation was as naught when set against the grievous loss of my wife. The entirely unexpected return of Holmes in April 1894, which I have related as "The Empty House" did something to fill the void caused by her death, but I had no intention of abandoning my practice until the grotesque events which I am about to relate.

One morning in May 1894, I was running my surgery. Anstruther had again asked me to minister his patients as he wanted to have a day away. It was therefore a weary look I gave my trusted receptionist when she came into my consulting room to say that two men wanted to see me. I probably brightened when she opened the door to them and I saw that the first was the tawny-bearded Inspector Gregson. The other was a young man with dark features and a beard as florid as Gregson's. He was introduced to me as Dr Barker.

When Gregson shook my hand, I could see from a white and drawn look on his face that he had an unpleasant commission to carry out, but I had no idea what form it would take. The thickly bearded Dr Barker declined even to respond to my proffered hand.

"Dr Watson," Gregson said at last, "Dr Barker here is a medical doctor and a member of the Roman Catholic faith. As you know, cremation was legalised in this country about ten years ago. Its legalisation was strongly opposed by Dr Barker's church and he has been undertaking a study of its impact on the disposal of the bodies of the dead. He has come up with some highly disturbing figures about deaths in the Paddington area and we would like to discuss them with you. We have come to you first among the doctors in Paddington as you are known to us through your work with Mr Holmes."

"I am happy to help in any way I can," I said, and was startled to see Gregson avert his gaze before bidding Dr Barker to make his deposition.

"Although I am, as Inspector Gregson stated," said Barker, in a high, querulous tone, "a medical doctor, I do not in fact practise medicine. I am instead attached to the renowned actuary, the Society for Life Assurances, as their medical adviser. Much of my work is on the statistics relating to mortality and death rates and, over the years, I have used my combination of skills to perform a number of studies of my own."

"Pray continue."

"The largest cremation site in the country is in Woking in Surrey. I have examined the records of the people cremated there. Cremations have been carried out on all ages and all classes of people over the last ten years. The human body is made in God's likeness, so destroying it after the living spirit has left it is something I regard as an abomination. To my great disapproval, the number of people who choose to make their bodily remains subject to this treatment is increasing."

Barker's face contorted with anger during this disposition and we had to wait till he had calmed before he continued.

"Most of the dead come from London, with large numbers also from Woking itself and surrounding towns such as Windsor, Reading and Guildford. For each London parish and for the four conurbations I have identified, the proportions of young and old fall within statistical norms. Thus, adjusting for local demographics, from each locale we see similar proportions of babes, pregnant women and those advanced in years. There is only one group of people from one borough where the statistical norms are not complied with. That is for people between the ages of fifty and sixty from Paddington. They constitute twenty per cent of all the bodies cremated from Paddington. Elsewhere, the average is eight per cent. To put it at its simplest, one would expect between nine and fourteen people from Paddington between the ages of fifty and sixty to have been cremated in Woking over the last ten years. The actual figure is twenty-six."

"Statistical stratification of deaths in this parish is not my area of expertise," I said, with a shrug. "Maybe the borough has a particularly large proportion of people in that age group."

"My checks have taken all such factors into account by extensive use of census figures."

"So do you feel that there is some want in the medical care in Paddington for those in more advanced years, or that there is some peculiarity to the air or the water here that makes them disproportionately prone to demise?" I then realised that Barker's statistics were capable of quite another interpretation from that which I had initially thought he had in mind. "Or do you feel that the situation of Paddington, poor though it is, makes people live longer, so that a higher proportion of its inhabitants reach a more advanced age than is achieved elsewhere?"

"Well, that is what I am hoping you can tell us, Dr Watson," said Dr Barker, the look of ill-humour that had been on his face since his arrival at the surgery suddenly mingled with glee. "You signed four of the death certificates."

I half stood up at what I regarded as a slight on my patient care by Dr Barker and then sat down again. I looked at Gregson for some indication of support from him, but he stared bleakly back at me for a few seconds before he looked down at the floor.

"What are the names of deceased?" I asked at last, and my voice sounded hollow as it echoed round my consulting room.

"Their surnames were Briggs, Stratford, Higgins and Granger."

"Briggs and Higgins I can recall," I said. "They were quite well-to-do ladies who expired in the last outbreak of enteric fever. Stratford and Granger I do not recall. I shall have to ask my receptionist for their files."

My receptionist was summoned, but was unable to find any files related to Stratford and Granger.

With a look of malevolence, Barker produced the death certificates. They were dated 12 March 1893 and 2 January 1894. It was unquestionably my signature on the certificates, but my mind remained blank. At a loss, I referred to the personal diary I had been keeping and this jogged my memory.

"These were not my patients," I explained. "That is why I have no files on them. Both of these are men who expired suddenly in the surgery next door. Anstruther was called away on urgent summonses to attend to women in childbirth and his receptionist asked me to sign the death certificates. As I recall, both deaths were featureless. Next of kin were summoned to identify the bodies, which was an unpleasant task as the faces of both men bore the distorted features common in victims of death from heart-failure. I myself had no hesitation in concluding on looking at the medical notes of the deceased that Anstruther had left for me that this was the cause of death in both cases. Indeed, both men had had an appointment to see Anstruther because of weakness to the heart. Accordingly, I signed the death certificates without conducting a detailed investigation into the cause of death."

"So there was nothing untoward about any of the four deaths?"

"Certainly not!"

"And did you benefit from the deaths?" asked Barker with a malevolent look.

I had assumed that the inquiry I was facing was into my standards of record keeping and administration. I knew these left something to be desired, as in my previous medical experience as an army doctor, record keeping had not been a primary requirement. It was only now I realised the turn this investigation was taking.

"Dr Barker! That is an outrageous suggestion. If you have an accusation to make, kindly make it directly rather than by sordid implication!"

Gregson intervened. "I think, Dr Barker, you had better leave any interrogation to the police." He turned to me." Dr Watson, as you will understand, Dr Barker is raising a significant matter which we will have to investigate with all the local surgeries. I would stress, Doctor, that you are not at present in any sense a suspect, but rather someone who can, in the truest sense, help us with our enquiries." For all Gregson's emollient tone, the menace carried by his words was unmistakable. "Dr Watson," he continued, "can you from medical experience throw any light on why, amongst people being cremated in the Paddington area, such a high proportion are aged between fifty and sixty?"

But I had heard enough. "Gregson!" I exclaimed, rising to my feet,

"*Inspector* Gregson, please, Dr Watson—"

I ignored the interruption: "While I am always happy to help the police, I cannot do so when faced with vile insinuations based on statistics I have had no opportunity to validate. If you wish to charge me with an offence, please do so. Otherwise, I am not prepared to be interviewed by you unless in the presence of my solicitor."

"Very well, Dr Watson. You will be hearing from us," said Gregson as he and Barker left my consulting room. I closed my surgery for the day at the earliest opportunity and made straight for Baker Street.

I have quoted Holmes elsewhere as saying that he played the game for its own sake, but I felt that he pushed this objective attitude too far when his first comment at my predicament, was "How stimulating!" before hurrying on to say as an afterthought "Although obviously most disturbing for you." We sat down in our familiar armchairs on either side of the fireplace. "Steady your nerves, good doctor, with this cigar," he said, reaching into the coal scuttle to extract his box. "And perhaps a dash of spirits might be of assistance," he added, pointing to the corner bookcase behind me, where bottles of whisky and brandy were perched precariously on top of a book on rubber vulcanisation. Holmes then leant back in his chair, with his fingertips resting against each other. "So these deaths were quite featureless?"

"Each death is, for the family of the deceased, a tragedy," I said a trifle stiffly, for I felt repelled by Holmes's apparent indifference to my plight. "But Barker was treating multiple deaths as mere statistics."

"I shall look into the matter," said Holmes at length. "It is still quite early," he added looking at his watch. "If you wish to stay here while I am away, you may do so." In an instant he was gone.

I had no desire to return either to Paddington or to Kensington, so I resolved to remain in the surroundings of Baker Street, although I knew not at what time Holmes might return. It was soothing to see the piles of documents in each corner, the Persian slipper where I knew Holmes kept his tobacco, and his unanswered correspondence, transfixed by a jack-knife at the centre of the wooden mantelpiece. The afternoon dragged, however, and at about three, I resolved to go back to Paddington and left a message for Holmes telling him where I was.

Rather to my surprise, the hour had advanced to no more than five o'clock in the evening when Holmes appeared. "I have made some progress with the case," he said, "although the matter is far from a simple one. A will is a public document, so I went to the Public Record Office to see to whom the four people whose death certificates you signed had made bequests."

"And?"

"You said that Stratford and Granger were Dr Anstruther's patients and from the poorer classes of society. It is perhaps no surprise that they left no wills. Their estates, if there were any assets at all, would have been divided up according to the laws of intestacy and you demonstrably would not have benefited from these. Mrs Briggs and Mrs Higgins left wills and made no mention of you. Therefore, there is no motive for seeking their deaths that can be ascribed to you."

"So to what do you attribute their deaths?"

"Dr Barker has undoubtedly identified a statistically significant irregularity in the number of deaths among fifty- to sixty-year-olds in the Paddington area who are then cremated. I looked at records of burials as opposed to cremations in the boroughs across London. It was noticeable that people in the fifty-to-sixty age group were slightly under-represented, but the number of burials is much larger than the number of cremations so it is not clear whether the under-representation is an insignificant deviation from the mean death rate, a statistical quirk, or a reflection of the higher number of people in that age group being cremated."

"Were you able to look into any of the other deaths to which Barker referred?"

"As you might imagine, most of the deaths in an area like Paddington came from a class of people whose demise left no material documentation. In most cases, there was no will because they had not thought to make one and there were, in any case, no assets to pass down. In the few cases where I found wills, no bequest was made to any physician. If a crime has been committed, then it would appear to be quite unique in that it would be heinous in its gravity, prolific in its quantity, untraceable in its execution and motiveless in its outcome."

"So what is there for us to do?"

"I am not sure that there is anything for us to do. There is no evidence to charge you with any offence and, from what I have seen, there is no evidence to charge anyone else with any offence either. I have no reason to think you will hear from either Gregson or Barker again. I would, nevertheless, in your position, display considerable caution in your handling of your patients who have deceased. Furthermore, I would, above all, not sign death certificates on behalf of other doctors without performing a thorough investigation of the body. I would also advocate that you focus increased attention on your administration. While there is unlikely to be a criminal investigation against you, I would not rule out the possibility of the British Council of Physicians taking an interest in your affairs."

I thought about the chaotic state in which Holmes continued to keep the quarters I used to share with him. "You are fortunate," I commented, "that there is no British Council of Detectives."

"I have always maintained that I am the world's only consulting detective," said Holmes a little quickly. "Accordingly I have no need of a trade association to determine an acceptable level of record keeping."

I decided to return to my living quarters in Kensington and went with Holmes to the door and down the stairs leading up from the street. We were just about to go our separate ways when Inspector Gregson and Dr Barker came round the corner.

I was unsure what to make of this and ignored their presence, but Holmes appeared anxious to engage them in discussion. "Still following your statistical friend, Gregson?" he asked.

"I have certainly been to a lot of surgeries today, Mr Holmes." replied Gregson with a weary look on his face. "In the absence of Dr Anstruther this morning, Dr Barker wanted to visit every other surgery in Paddington, though he chose the most inconvenient route possible to get around them."

Barker had been about to bang on Anstruther's door, presumably in the hope that the latter had returned, but, perhaps alerted by the discussions at the foot of his stairs, Dr Anstruther himself, tall, lean and bespectacled, opened the door before Barker could knock. "Would you gentlemen like to come in?" he asked politely.

But it was Holmes who answered, saying: "It is very good to have the chance to talk to you, Dr Anstruther. We would be delighted to speak to you. Come Watson," he said, turning to me, "I would not wish to continue this investigation without my Boswell."

I don't think Barker and Gregson had anticipated that Holmes and I would join them in their investigation of Paddington's doctors, but Gregson made no move to stop us. The four of us went through the bare and gloomy hallway of Anstruther's house into an equally Spartan consulting room. Barker made the same sorts of accusatory remarks to Anstruther as he had made to me. My neighbour had signed no fewer than twelve of the death certificates of the people whose deaths Barker regarded as suspicious.

"And what is the nature of your concern, Dr Barker?" asked Anstruther, leaning back in his chair and apparently displaying none of the outrage that I had felt when Barker had made his accusations to me. "You appear to have nothing of substance." He paused to light a cigarette and bluish-grey puffs of smoke rose lazily into the air around him. "You have found a statistical anomaly, but statistics throw up anomalies all the time and the sorts of population sizes you are talking about are barely significant."

I could see Barker redden under his beard at Anstruther's dismissive response and the latter pressed home his advantage:

"You have no body that will betray any symptoms of foul play since all the deaths you regard with such concern have resulted in cremations. Given that my patients were of modest means, you cannot claim I have benefitted from their deaths. The statistics may indicate an abnormality, but I can assure you that there was none in any of the cases under investigation. Why, I even let a fellow doctor, the good Watson here, sign off the death certificates of two of my patients, which I would surely not do if there were anything untoward about the deaths. Dr Barker, you are surely not accusing me of eliminating these people for the sheer pleasure of—" he paused as he sought a suitable expression, "—terminating their existence?"

There was something slightly repellent and at the same time impenetrable about my neighbour's serenity as he repeated the same arguments that Holmes had used to suggest there was no case to answer. As though reading my thoughts, Dr Anstruther leant back in his chair. "I have no case to answer, no case to answer—" he leant forward and stubbed out his still-glowing cigarette in the ashtray before him, "—at all."

A few minutes later we found ourselves on the street – Barker fulminating at Gregson that nothing of substance had been achieved that day – before we went our separate ways.

The next morning, I determined to ignore the events of the previous day and went to my practice early to try and remedy some of the administrative deficiencies to which my attention had been drawn. It was when I was due to see my first patient at nine o'clock that my receptionist came in to ask if I could take Anstruther's patients for the day.

"Is he away again?" I asked wearily.

"No, Doctor Watson," she replied. "He was knocked over and killed by a milk cart early this morning as he was going to get his newspaper."

I could hardly close my surgery for a second successive day under these circumstances, but my attempts to minister to patients were soon interrupted by the arrival of Gregson, Barker and Holmes.

Gregson explained for my benefit that Anstruther had stepped out into the road without looking and been struck down by a heavily laden carriage pulled by Shire horses. Death had been instantaneous.

"I wonder if the death was an accident, or whether he killed himself after yesterday's barely concealed accusations from Dr Barker. He struck me as being very far from the type who would shy from combat," mused Holmes. "Anstruther had a lifestyle out of keeping with the income from his practice and yet we have no evidence that this had anything to do with the high level of deaths at his practice."

"We need to refer to medical experts here," I opined. "I think we should go to the British Council of Physicians in Grantly Square to take advantage of their expertise."

Dr Antony-Ball, Head of the Council, was known as a fierce defender of members' interests. I doubt that he could have been prevailed upon to see me on my own, but the name of Holmes on a visiting card had the characteristic effect of persuading a man in authority to grant us an interview. I gave Dr Antony-Ball a summary of events with assistance from Holmes, Barker and Gregson.

"Dr Watson," responded Antony-Ball, "your line of enquiry seems directed towards denigrating a fellow doctor who, due to today's tragic events, can no longer defend himself. I can only speculate as to your motives, but the hope of getting your former neighbour's patients by default is a plausible one. The Council takes very seriously the need for our members to have administrative procedures that are beyond reproach. And by your own admission, you have signed a death certificate on behalf of another doctor apparently without making any serious effort to investigate the cause of death."

For a second time in two days, my voice seemed to have a hollow ring to it as I felt I was being cast in the role of the accused when my role was that of a witness. "I did not come here to discuss the shortcomings of my own practice. I came here to express my concerns about a neighbouring practice."

"From what you say, there is nothing to investigate in your neighbouring practice. There is no admission there of administrative shortcomings and none will be forthcoming, given Dr Anstruther's sudden demise. Dr Watson, you have come here as a baseless accuser, where it is in fact you whose working methods will require a full investigation from the Council. And you, Dr Barker," he said, turning to my first accuser, "have done the medical world no service by your investigations based on statistical analysis. Your ill-conceived conjectures have risked creating a wave of general unease around Paddington about the standard of medical care being provided when it is the interests and wellbeing of the individual patient that are paramount. Dr Watson, we will perform a full review into your administrative procedures. I can at this stage exclude no sanction. And you, Dr Barker, if you continue to ventilate these unfounded rumours against fellow doctors, your right to practise medicine will be withdrawn."

The review of my practice's administration was launched immediately and with the minimum of discretion. It soon became something of a *cause célèbre* in Paddington. My patients rapidly found other medical surgeries to meet their medical needs. It was soul-destroying to see the business I had worked so hard to build up, leach away. In "The Norwood Builder" I commented that

Holmes found money for a young relative of his, Verner, to buy my practice in the very first few months following his return, although I only became aware of his generosity after the event. My reader may have wondered how Holmes, who had not been earning major sums during his three-year absence from London, was able to fund such a purchase. In fact, there was very little money to find as, in the end, I was forced to sell the business at the written-down value of its assets with no goodwill at all. The subsequent loss of my practising certificate came only after this and was of little financial consequence to me as I had already thrown my lot in with Holmes. It was, nevertheless, a major blow to my self-esteem. Meanwhile, the Society for Life Assurances reviewed its business model and decided it no longer needed a full-time medical officer as it could get medical advice on an *ad hoc* basis from a panel of contracted doctors. Other actuaries subsequently made the same decision and Dr Barker was unable to get anyone to employ him.

Just as Holmes had not been overt in his sympathy over the loss of Mary, so his sympathy was muted over the loss of my practice. As he waited for his consulting business to rebuild following his return, I keened for the loss of my own business and found solace at the billiard table of my club. My reader may recall my billiard partner Thurston, about whom Holmes was to make a typically brilliant deduction at the time of the grave matter I have chronicled as "The Adventure of the Dancing Men". Thurston was a company promoter and would regularly try to interest me in shares in companies which were seeking a floatation. Normally the sums he was seeking were beyond my pocket but one evening, poised over a shot, Thurston straightened up and said:

"You know, Watson, there is a real opportunity for you to make some money from a business not far from where your practice used to be. The Paddington Brewery is a highly profitable company mainly owned by the Winsome family and they are looking to sell a large minority stake. I have a prospectus in my briefcase, which I shall give you at the conclusion of this frame."

My only previous investment with Thurston had been several years previously when he had interested me in the prospectus of a company which manufactured buttons. The prospectus had failed to disclose some of the liabilities the company had in respect of former long-standing employees. These were identified only when they vested two years after the floatation and the disclosure of them prompted a dramatic slide in the share price. My somewhat haphazard approach to finances meant that I had quite forgotten I owned the shares and the loss of capital only came to light when I was assessing my existing assets with a view to buying my Paddington practice. As a result of the experience I viewed Thurston's suggestion of an investment with circumspection.

I think Thurston saw my look of hesitancy and he re-assured me: "Although the Paddington Brewery is a long-established business, it has a predominantly young work-force to whom it has no obligations – I checked this with the main shareholder, whom I know well. You can invest with confidence in this business. When they float, there will be a significant premium on these shares and there will always be a demand for beer."

I mentioned Thurston's proposal and the outcome of my previous venture with Thurston when I was back at Baker Street. Holmes asked to look at the prospectus.

"It is curious," he commented after a brief examination of the balance sheet, "that a large business like the Paddington Brewery has no pension obligations at all. Recent company legislation requires such liabilities to be stated in the company's accounts and in any prospectus – just as you had to disclose your pension obligation to your receptionist when you sold your practice."

"Indeed," I commented grimly. "The lengthening of anticipated lifespans made my pension obligation to my receptionist much the biggest liability on my business's balance sheet and that, along with the precipitous decline in takings as a result of the investigation by the British Council of Physicians, is why the proceeds on its sale were so small."

"Who are the current shareholders of the Paddington Brewery who are looking to sell a stake?"

"I understand that it is a predominantly family-owned business but the full listing of shareholders is disclosed at the back."

We were surprised to see that amongst the shareholders listed on the last page of the prospectus was the widow of Dr Anstruther. This discovery prompted a sharp intake of breath from Holmes.

"A motive at last for the high death rates in Paddington!" He exclaimed. "When we were looking at Dr Barker's scandalous accusation, I was unable to find any motive that Dr Anstruther might have had in respect of the death of any of the people whose death certificates he signed. I do, however, recall that three of them had worked for the Paddington Brewery. This was not a great surprise to me as the brewery is the largest business in Paddington. These deaths occurred just before the deceased attained pensionable age. The company clearly replaced them with young employees, who could be offered a much less costly money purchase scheme rather than a pension based on their final pay. This is a very material motive for a shareholder in the brewery. And you will remember that we were unable to account for the doctor's apparent financial well-being in spite of the fact that his practice seemed to have an even slower turnover of patients than yours. The dividends from this stake will have been a major source of income for Dr Anstruther."

Holmes said no more that evening, but he disappeared for the next two days. It was at lunchtime of the third day when he reappeared. The gleam in his eye told me that he had made progress in his investigations, which was confirmed as we sat down to our midday repast.

"This case has its inception from our case in Birmingham several years ago and, while I have not found enough to go before a jury, I am making progress in finding enough to put before Dr Antony-Ball."

"But Holmes, the matter is closed. I have lost my practice, Dr Barker has lost his livelihood. We must all make the best of the situation, as I seek to do in selling my works about you and in looking for suitable investments."

"Our investigation to date," continued Holmes, seeming not to hear my wan expression of despair, "had failed to find a motive for the high number of deaths among Dr Anstruther's patients, or an obvious means for him to carry out killings with so little fear of detection that he let you sign death certificates. But my research among the companies around Paddington has shown me that Anstruther had holdings in several of them."

"But why would that provide him with a motive for killing his patients?"

“They all had generous pension schemes based on the final salary of the employee. By killing the more mature employees before they could claim their pensions, he removed a substantial liability from the companies of which he was a shareholder and thereby increased the value of his stakes as well as removing the cost of pension contributions from those companies’ outgoings.”

“Is that not somewhat fanciful?” I responded. “Have you a means that is more tangible?”

“I cannot deny that my theory for a motive is speculation. But having found a possible motive, I then started to speculate about the means.”

For all my friend’s normal dispassionate air in his dealings with me, my reader will appreciate how grateful I was to have him on my side in my struggle to regain my professional reputation.

“And have you got something, Holmes?”

“Only an inkling,” he replied. “I was struck when we were in Anstruther’s practice that for all the artistic interests you ascribed to him, the walls of his practice were bare of any paintings, and when I looked up his will at the Public Record Office there were no paintings in his effects. Let us see what the Paddington art-supplies shop knows about Dr Anstruther. Please leave the talking to me, Watson. I am going to present myself as the solicitor acting on behalf of the widow of Dr Anstruther’s and will present you as my clerk. I would advise you, Doctor, that you may hear things in this interview you do not like. I would beg you not to respond."

In my eagerness to redeem my name, I confess I only half-heard my friend's last remark. As my reader will discover, it was fortunate indeed that I did not miss it altogether.

We were soon at Adams & Johns, a shop round the corner from Dr Anstruther's practice. The shop proprietor, Mr Johns, was standing behind the counter as we came through the door. Holmes introduced himself as Mr Grove, senior partner at Grove, Grove, Perry & Co and introduced me as Mr Wilson, the firm's senior clerk.

"In the course of my duties to Dr Anstruther's widow," Holmes told Mr Johns, "I have been going through his effects. As you will understand, she is still too distraught by events to be able to do much. During my compilation of an inventory of Dr Anstruther's assets, I came across a large amount of paint for artwork which I assume you supplied him with as you are the only supplier of this type of material in Paddington."

"A tragic case, the death of Dr Anstruther," said Mr Johns, a tall man with an Irish accent. "Such a kind man. Always out at his patients, always listening to their cares. We had him as our doctor and often he came to us rather than us going to him. And that saved us going to the apothecary. He always believed in injections, did Dr

Anstruther, which he would give to us on the spot. A bodkin was never out of his hands. I never went to his neighbour, Dr Farquhar, or to Dr Farquhar's successor. I always heard that at that practice they simply told you to go and get some pills."

I was about to open my mouth to interject when I felt Holmes's heel stab into my shin and remembered his injunction to remain silent.

"To realise as much as I can for the estate," continued Holmes, "I want to see how much this paint is worth. There are three large boxes containing tubes of it at his house and I wanted to form a view on whether the paint has a disposal value."

"A very keen painter, Dr Anstruther, God bless him," said Mr Johns thoughtfully. "Always busy painting seascapes and cloudscapes. It's easy for me to tell you how much his paint cost him because he was the only customer for the Prussian Blue which I ordered in specially for him. Most of my other customers only bought paints for their children or for painting local scenes. Let's have a look at his account and see what I charged him for it. I might be able to do his widow a favour. Seems only right."

He reached up to a shelf behind him and got down a large file. He pulled out several invoices to Dr Anstruther, all containing details of purchases of Prussian Blue with some small amounts of other paints. Eventually he straightened himself up:

"I can try to see if I can get my supplier to take it back. I can offer you one guinea a box for it. Prussian Blue is an expensive paint to make, though it is not all that often used unless you're doing what Dr Anstruther was doing."

"Thank you," said Holmes gravely. "This may be of some comfort to poor Mrs Anstruther."

We emerged from the shop and once we were out of earshot I turned angrily to Holmes:

"So what did that show us? All we confirmed was that Anstruther bought blue paint for his skyscapes and you gave yet another person the opportunity to traduce me."

"On the contrary, dear Watson, the invoices have given us a major weapon in our battle to restore your professional reputation."

"So Anstruther bought paint. What else?" I retorted, barely able to rein in my fury.

"Precisely, Watson," soothed Holmes. "What kind of painter has need of paints, but no need for brushes, canvasses and other art requisites? Paint was the only thing on any of the invoices that Adams showed to us."

I may have looked even more blank than usual at what my friend was clearly regarding as a major coup. So Holmes continued:

"Prussian Blue pigment – the main paint that Anstruther bought – is what is used to make cyanide. That is why Hydrogen Cyanide is sometimes called prussic acid. I would speculate that making cyanide was what he was using the Prussian Blue for and that is why paint was the only thing Anstruther bought at the art-supplies shop. That is also why we can find no paintings."

"So that was why he was happy for me to sign off two of the death certificates!" I exclaimed, realising at last the importance of Holmes's deduction. "Death by cyanide poisoning produces distorting of the facial features very similar to distortions caused by death from heart disease, and the medical notes of the two deceased both had references to treatments for heart problems. Accordingly, it was easy for me to read the medical notes of Anstruther's patients and ascribe the deaths to heart failure rather than looking for any outside cause. And the cremation of the bodies would mean that any evidence of foul play would be destroyed!" I said with mounting excitement.

"And Dr Anstruther's preference for visiting his patients also explains why his stairs were so little worn. His practice may have been more profitable than I surmised on the way back from Birmingham after the capture of Beddington."

"So, Holmes, what are to be your next moves?"

"No, good Doctor, what do you want your next moves to be?"

I looked into the eyes of my friend. "As a matter of personal pride, I would like to have a practising certificate again even if I do not work as a doctor."

"Then let us go and see Dr Antony-Ball."

When we arrived at the British Council of Physicians, Dr Antony-Ball at first declined to see us. It was only when Holmes said we would not leave until he saw us that we were granted an interview.

"Have you anything new to say, Mr Holmes?" asked Antony-Ball.

"I have indications, Doctor Antony-Ball, promising indications."

"Indications – promising, or otherwise, though your choice of adjective seems wildly inappropriate for an investigation of the kind you seem to be conducting – hardly provide a reason why I should prolong an interview with you, Mr Holmes."

Holmes explained how he had identified not only a plausible financial motive for Dr Anstruther to have ended the lives of his patients once they had reached a certain age, but also a clue as to the means he had used.

"You are merely adding speculation to the speculative work of a now-discredited statistician on a matter where the only person who could have definitive knowledge of what happened is dead. It is not therefore possible to form an opinion on the validity of your accusations. The means you suggest that Dr Anstruther used are unprovable and the motives you suggest, flimsy," said Antony-Ball flushing with anger. "I decline to enter into conjectural discussions."

"So you are refusing to agree to any sort of investigation into a matter of the utmost gravity?"

"To conduct any sort of investigation into your accusations will only give them an unwarranted credibility among the more suggestible of our fellow citizens and they will be used to blacken the name of every doctor in the land."

We had reached an impasse and I was preparing to gather up my things to go.

"Are you aware of the literary successes of my friend?" asked Holmes.

"I confess I can see no reason why I should follow the literary career of a struck-off doctor."

"My friend's works are widely read, Dr Antony-Ball, widely read. I am sure that he could make a most entertaining tale about a disproportionate number of deaths in Paddington, the reluctance of the British Council of Physicians to investigate them, and the treatment of those who had the courage to raise their concerns. And since you yourself regard the matter as trivial, the main speculations could be written so as to appeal to as wide an audience as possible."

"Mr Holmes! I represent the affairs of every registered doctor in the country. Each doctor I represent has passed an arduous program of examinations to be a fit representative of the medical profession. As far as I can observe from your line of questioning, both now and at our previous interview, you carry out your investigations through ill-founded allegations proper to a gutter journalist using the restricted mind-set of a bookkeeper."

"Dr Antony-Ball, you have ended the medical livelihood of both my colleague, Dr Watson, here and also of Dr Barker. Your refusal to conduct any sort of investigation into these allegations and your treatment of those who have raised them seems to be motivated by the desire to protect the reputation of your organisation's members rather than to defend the interests of patients."

"I am not prepared to start a witch-hunt against my brother doctors based on the insubstantial evidence you are providing of malpractice in one surgery out of thousands."

"You state, Dr Antony-Ball," replied Holmes, "that I have the investigative methods of a sensation-seeking journalist and the intellect of a bookkeeper. Let me put it to you that far from being an obstacle to my investigation, these qualities allayed to the literary talents of my friend and the statistical skills of Dr Barker, are precisely what are needed for us to progress in this case. Dr Barker is at a loose end. Dr Watson has a following as a writer. I am sure Dr Barker could be asked to conduct investigations into death rates at any practice in the country and Dr Watson would have nothing to lose in providing commentaries of a most prurient nature to the popular press. You could, of course, refuse to conduct a properly funded and resourced investigation of your own. A headline in the popular press to this effect would sell a lot of newspapers. 'BCP bigwig: no investigation into high death rates' would make a good opener."

"I had no idea that attempted blackmail played so prominent a part in your successes," said Antony-Ball, flushing to the roots of his hair.

"In a good cause I am a practitioner of many of the so-called dark arts," responded Holmes. "Let me, therefore, add the skills of a cleric to those of the bookkeeper and the journalist. Dr Antony-Ball, in the words of St Luke, I would say to you, every hair on your head is counted and that your head of hair is as false as your defence of your members' vested interests. While a first headline may say

‘BCP bigwig: no investigation into high death rates’, a subsequent headline may confirm that the term bigwig is even more an indication of falsity than it appears at first sight.”

Antony-Ball stood up and then sat down. As he did so, I could see that his thick head of hair had a seam which was, as is always the case once Holmes points a matter out, childishly obvious.

There was a brief silence while Antony-Ball recovered his composure. When he had done so, he informed us of proposals under consideration by the British Council of Physicians. Under these, all cases where practising certificates had been withdrawn would be subject to automatic review after three years. This proposal was likely to be accepted by the Board of the Council at its next meeting. “This is information that I am giving to you in the strictest confidence and I would not expect you to make any report of the discussions that the three of us have had in any outlet. You will also understand,” Antony-Ball continued, “that this development has been under discussion from a time long pre-dating your Paddington investigation, just as you should be aware that I have not been in any way swayed by any of your submissions.”

By the time my practising certificate was finally restored to me, I had already concluded that earning money as a writer of short stories was far more remunerative than life as a doctor. It was thus to be many years and after my second marriage before I was to go back into the profession. But shortly after the events described above, I chanced to meet Dr Barker on Baker Street. Although he still bore the thick, dark beard of our first encounter, his whole demeanour bespoke bonhomie as he told me he was shortly due to travel to Rome, where the Roman Catholic church had asked him to conduct an investigation into the correlation between undertaking pilgrimages and achieving medical outcomes beyond the normal range of expectations.

"After going to Rome, I will need to visit many of the sites associated with miracles," he said. "I shall go to Assisi, Santiago de Compostela and Lourdes. I may even go to Walsingham at some point, even though that site is quite tarnished by the Anglican usurpation of the Roman church."

I cautiously expressed my pleasure at his change of fortune and he added:

"It is high time that the church sought to prove a statistical link between visiting shrines and recovery from conditions untreatable even by the wonders of modern science." He continued: "For me, it is an extraordinary opportunity. One minute I was unable to find a position of any sort, and the next minute I can apply my statistical skills to a matter of the greatest personal and public interest. As someone who is a devout adherent of my faith, it is hard indeed not to speculate that the hand of a higher power is behind this."

The Red Priest's Treasure Trove

After the adventure of 1903, which I have previously narrated under the title "The Priory School", Holmes increasingly withdrew from active criminal detective work. This was not due to any want of demand for his services either from Scotland Yard or from private clients, but rather because Holmes's investigative skills were sought in spheres other than crime – in particular those of science and music. As Holmes was an expert in both, it was not surprising that he often gave priority to commissions arising from these disciplines. My reader will be unsurprised to learn, if he has not guessed already, that many of the ground-breaking scientific and musical discoveries made in the first ten years of this twentieth century were the direct result of Holmes's change of focus.

Towards the end of 1903, Holmes was approached by the scientist Albert Einstein, who was having difficulties with his work on the photo-electric effect. Holmes was able to clarify two points on the effect of gravity on light for the great scientist, ironically basing part of his own work on "The Dynamics of an Asteroid" by Professor Moriarty. This led directly to Einstein's *annus mirabilis* in 1905 when he published four great papers which eventually resulted in him being awarded the Nobel Prize for Physics in 1922.

Holmes's connection with Albert Einstein had an unexpected side-effect. The great scientist recommended Holmes's investigative skills to his cousin, the Mozart expert, Alfred Einstein. The latter had been trying without success to track down a score for an oboe concerto by Mozart, which the composer had referred to in a letter to his father, but for which no parts were known. Holmes was already a proud possessor of Breitkopf and Härtel's Mozart Complete Edition and was rapidly able to direct Alfred Einstein's attention to the score of Mozart's Flute Concerto in D Major in which the violin part never got lower than the second-lowest tone of each string. To Holmes, this demonstrated that it had been transposed up one tone from an earlier piece in C major. Holmes suggested that the earlier piece may in fact have been the oboe concerto and that Mozart was looking for an easy way to complete a commission for a flute concerto which he found uncongenial. The parts of the original oboe concerto were subsequently found in Salzburg in 1921.

In 1907, the musicologist Lothar Percher approached Holmes. Percher was of the opinion that the work published as Mozart's Symphony Number Thirty-Seven as part of the Complete Edition referred to above, was stylistically much closer to the music of Michael Haydn, the younger brother of the more famous Josef

Haydn, than to that of Mozart. Percher was making a study of Michael Haydn's music and consequently was intimately acquainted with the latter's music of which he subsequently published a catalogue of works.

Holmes examined the score and concluded that while the slow introduction of the work was indeed by Mozart, it appeared to have been appended to a work of a different provenance. He suggested to Percher that he search for a work with the same incipit as the fast section of the first movement. A Michael Haydn's Symphony in G Major was soon confirmed as the origin of all but the opening of Mozart's so-called Symphony Number Thirty-Seven.

My friend's discovery about Mozart's Symphony Number Thirty-Seven naturally caused major embarrassment to Breitkopf and Härtel, the world's oldest music publisher, who had already numbered four later symphonies as numbers Thirty-Eight to Forty-One. They declined to change the later numbers but Holmes's discovery meant that Mozart's so-called Symphony Number Thirty-Seven has become a *rara avis* or rare bird in our concert halls. Holmes declined to have his name associated with this discovery or any of the other musical or scientific discoveries that he had made, although he did quip in Newtonian fashion on his unmasking of the true writer of Mozart's Symphony Number Thirty-Seven: "If I have seen further than Breitkopf and Härtel, maybe it is because I have taken the trouble to read the full score of the symphony before declaring it to be by Mozart."

Holmes's success as a musical investigator should not, perhaps, be considered unexpected. Holmes was a rare performer indeed on the violin and a composer of no small merit. Already, in 1895, he had caused a stir in musical circles by publishing a monograph on the polyphonic motets of the Dutch composer Lassus, which had been declared by experts to be the last word on the subject. These musical accomplishments, allied to his unsurpassed forensic and investigative skills, equipped him better than a professional musician for solving the many mysteries of the world of Classical music.

Some of his musicological investigations, like some of his criminal cases, led nowhere. This was often because the passage of time had left no lasting trail of what had happened, or because a work he was searching for – the complete version of Schubert's Unfinished Symphony is an obvious case in point – had never been written. These cases were often amongst the most interesting ones, but it is hard to present them without frustrating the reader with a story that has a beginning but no end. At the time, I thought Holmes's 1907 investigation into the circumstances behind the writing of Bach's Brandenburg concerti was going to fall into this incomplete category. Holmes had been commissioned by the Leipzig-based Bachgesellschaft or Bach Society to try to unravel a mystery which Holmes elucidated to me in his customarily succinct manner:

"It's like this, Watson: The history of the Classical concerto is fairly well established. Antonio Vivaldi, a Venetian, who was often known as the Prete rosso or the 'red priest' because he was a priest with red hair, was the first person to popularise the genre of the virtuoso concerto. That is a piece where a solo instrument or sometimes more than one instrument is pitted against a whole orchestra. He published a set of twelve concerti under the title of L'estro armonico or 'Harmonic Inspiration' in Amsterdam in about 1712. This collection included four such concerti for solo violin and four for two violins accompanied by a four-part string orchestra, although these and other concerti of his had circulated earlier in manuscript. The works are amongst the most influential pieces of music in European music history. Bach transcribed some of them for keyboard, Handel imitated their construction in his organ concerti, and there is a direct bloodline from them to the concerti of Mozart, Beethoven and Brahms, which continue to dominate the programmes of our concert halls. Allow me to play you some Vivaldi, whose music you will never have heard before."

He placed his violin under his chin and started to play.

Under his fingers rose a sound world unlike any other I had heard.

I was used to Holmes playing Mendelsohn lieder and Sarasate show pieces, but the music of Vivaldi had a ferocious energy mingled with a melodic sweetness all of its own. I was utterly beguiled and when at length Holmes came to a halt, I was lost for breath – far more so than Holmes was. I had almost forgotten that the objective of the investigation was Bach.

I put this to Holmes, who said "Ah, my dear Watson, this is only the starting point of the mystery. In 1721, Bach sent a collection of six concerti of his own to the Margrave of Brandenburg, the ruler of a small city-state just outside Berlin. He attached a letter in French to the Margrave which makes it seem probable that he was seeking an appointment or a commission using the concerti as his calling card. He had met the Margrave face to face on a previous occasion. These six so-called Brandenburg concerti are magnificent in their own way," and here Holmes broke off to play a jaunty gigue, which he told me was the opening of the last movement of the fifth concerto of the set. "But they are also magnificently different from any other concerti that had been written before and, I would posit, from any since."

He paused to play a few more measures of the gigue.

"Before Vivaldi," he continued, "there was really no such thing as a virtuoso concerto. Previously, ensemble works were described as concerti to distinguish them from pieces for voices, and were sequences of dance movements where groups of instrumentalists were put together without the objective of showing off the abilities of one or two performers. After Vivaldi, the style of an abstract three-movement piece showing off a soloist or soloists became more or less de rigeur. Bach's Brandenburg concerti take Vivaldi's concept and stretch both its form and virtuosic requirements far more than he or any of his contemporaries ever attempted, and far more than anyone else has done since."

"But you have always said that the music of Bach is the closest thing there is to human perfection, so Bach was capable of doing whatever he wanted."

"That is so, but let me outline to you how extreme this stretching of form and instrumentation is. The first concerto adopts the form of a three-movement concerto with a very large ensemble and then adds on a number of dance movements of no special distinction. The second concerto calls for a trumpet player of a skill far beyond that required by any trumpet music that Bach ever wrote before or afterwards – and he wrote many trumpet parts – and far beyond any other trumpet part written in the next hundred years. After that, the trumpet became subject to numerous technical modifications to make it easier to play. The third concerto is for nine-part strings. At this time, most ensembles could only stretch to four string players. This piece also calls upon the nine players to improvise a slow movement – a freedom composers do not give their performers for the obvious reason that it would be beyond the capability of even the most talented ensembles. The fourth concerto calls for a violinist of staggering brilliance while the fifth concerto requires a keyboard player of similarly preternatural virtuosity. The sixth concerto eschews violins entirely and is for violas and cellos."

"Is this really such a mystery?" I asked. "Surely Bach was responding to a commission from the Margrave and was following his instructions?"

"Your response is, of course, the logical explanation, but consider this: Because King Frederick William I of Prussia was not a significant patron of the arts, the Margrave lacked the musicians in his ensemble to perform the concertos. The parts of the music were sold for a pittance after the Margrave's death and the autograph manuscript of the concerti was only rediscovered in the archives of the Brandenburg court in 1849. It was obvious that it had never been used and, given the peculiarities I have described, this is not very surprising."

"Could Bach have been trying to show what he could do? Perhaps these concerti were written for the ensemble he was used to writing for, and his plan was to demonstrate his skills by playing the solo violin and keyboard parts of the fourth and fifth concerti himself?"

"That may be admissible," conceded Holmes. "But that leaves so much unexplained. Why would he send a Margrave, who almost certainly could not read a score, a paper demonstration of his skills as a composer, including two pieces out of six which required Bach himself, who lived eighty miles away in Cöthen, in Saxony, to perform them? Why did he send the other four pieces? We know of no major musical figure working at the Margrave's court who could have evaluated Bach's music or performed the more difficult pieces. Equally, Bach cannot have taken the trouble to write out six elaborate concerti in manuscript, merely so that the Margrave could display them on his wall, or as a practical joke. There must have been some other motivation for Bach doing as he did. His motivation in writing the Brandenburg concerti in the way that he did is what the Bach Society is asking me to investigate."

"So what are you proposing to do now?" I asked.

For answer, Holmes reached up to the shelf and started to take down a selection of volumes from the recently published Complete Edition of Bach's music. "The Bach Society has given me all forty-six volumes of their publication as an advance payment for solving this mystery, and as a tool to enable me to study Bach's music at its source. This is a reward far more munificent than any other I have ever received for my work, since Bach's music is an inexhaustible treasury of glories. I would add," he said with a slightly sly smile, "that the reward for completing the commission is on a similarly lavish scale."

For the rest of the day he sat entirely absorbed over the music, interrupting his study of the scores only to get down more volumes. Occasionally he could be heard sighing with pleasure at some particular felicity in Bach's work and sometimes he put his violin to his chin to play a strain or two of the notes in front of him.

At the end of the day he turned to me: "My examination of these scores merely increases the mystery. Many of the movements from the Brandenburg concerti appear in reworked form in other pieces by Bach. Yet in all cases they are reworked without the eccentricities to which I previously alluded, making them straightforward for an ordinary ensemble to perform. The more extreme oddities – such as the stratospheric trumpet part – do not appear at all, or, in the case of the coruscating cadenza for keyboard in the fifth concerto, appear only in a greatly simplified form. I am not clear whether these other versions of the music were written before or after 1721, but it is clear that Bach was aware both of the lasting value of his material and the performance difficulty of what he had produced. If there is one thing that can be relied on in a composer, it is his practical sense in producing versions of his music that can actually be performed. Yet, practical man though Bach undoubtedly was, he sent this manuscript to Brandenburg, although its technical difficulties rendered it unperformable there."

Holmes subsequently travelled to both Brandenburg and Cöthen to investigate the mystery further, but his findings merely made matters still more inexplicable. He told me afterwards how he had searched through the court archives of Brandenburg to find payments to musicians and had found a few to string players, none to any wind players, and none to any composer he recognised. In Cöthen he found that the regular ensemble under Bach's charge had seventeen players which corresponded approximately in number but not necessarily in instrumentation to the ensembles needed for the six concerti, apart from the first. As Holmes pointed out, however, this merely made matters stranger as why would Bach send a manuscript adapted to his Cöthen ensemble to Brandenburg and not retain a copy for use in Cöthen?

My last question to him about the Brandenburg concerti was not about Bach at all but about Vivaldi. Bach, I knew, had died in Leipzig in 1750. What had happened to Vivaldi, I asked Holmes.

"No one is quite sure," said Holmes. "He is known to have died in poverty in Vienna in 1741 having composed music for a girls' orphanage in Venice for many years. Aside from the works that were published in his lifetime and which lie gathering dust in specialist music libraries, there is no music of his available to the public, so today his music is known only to the ear of God. And, just as very little of Bach's work was printed in his life time, so it is likely that most of Vivaldi's music was left in manuscript form. But the location of his manuscripts, if indeed any are extant, is unknown. The pieces I have played to you are my own arrangements for violin of the works that Bach had arranged for keyboard and that is the only way to hear any of his music."

Holmes picked up his violin and played some more violin music by Vivaldi transcribed by Bach for keyboard and re-transcribed for violin by Holmes himself.

And that was our last discussion on the topic, for other matters arose which meant that Holmes could not continue the investigation.

By early 1927, I had quite forgotten the whole mystery. I remarried in 1907 and from then on I was busy in practice and heard only very occasionally and very irregularly from Holmes from his retirement home on the South Downs. I had just completed a long round of patient visits and was writing up my notes when the maid knocked and said "There's a visitor to see you, sir."

"The practice is now closed and will remain so until I return from holiday in a week. My neighbour has already agreed to take my patients over that time. Ask him to call there tomorrow."

A familiar voice boomed from behind the door: "I'm sure Dr Watson will make an exception for this visitor."

My heart leapt. "Holmes!" I cried "How splendid that you are here!" Holmes came into my consulting room. He was still thin to gaunt in form, but his eye was as piercing as ever. To my considerable surprise, he was carrying his violin case.

"I never saw you look better," said he. "And I can strongly recommend to you your planned trip to Venice for your twentieth wedding anniversary."

The Continental railway timetable was open on my desk and Holmes had attended our wedding, but even so, the ease with which he deduced what was to have been a surprise for my wife took my breathe away. I confessed to him as much.

"And what brings you to London?" I asked.

"I have an appointment in a few minutes with an Italian musicologist called Alberto Gentili. That is why I have also brought my violin. He has kindly agreed to call here so that we can talk. As my much-valued chronicler, you are of course free to join us if you wish."

I must confess my jaw dropped at Holmes's presumption in organising a meeting with a complete stranger at my house without asking me first, but assented to his wishes as I have always done. This example of his presumption was, in any case, shortly to be followed by one of much greater magnitude and personal impact.

"So what does this Italian musicologist want to see you for?" I asked.

"I confess I have no idea, except that he telegraphed me to say that he was coming to London on a matter of the greatest importance and wanted, before anyone else, to speak to me."

A few minutes later, the maid brought in Dr Gentili, a tall, elegant man in his mid-fifties, who spoke excellent English. After introductions, he came straight to the point.

"In the autumn of last year, the administrators of a boarding school in Piedmont run by the Salesian Fathers discovered in their archives a large number of old music manuscripts which they wanted to sell to pay for building repairs. They called upon the National Library in Turin to value the material and the library passed the matter to me as I am professor of music history at Turin University. I have frequently been asked to perform such a task, and frequently the manuscripts prove to be no more interesting than family song books or old, hand-written copies of works already in wide public circulation. I asked for a list and suggested that the material be sent to Turin so that I could inspect it carefully. When the crates arrived, I opened the first one up." Dr Gentili stopped as though overcome by an overwhelming emotion. "Inside were innumerable volumes of autograph manuscripts of an Italian composer of the early eighteenth century called Antonio Vivaldi."

By this time my friendship with Holmes dated back over forty years, but on this occasion, for the first time in our long collaboration, there was a look of unalloyed joy on his face. There was a seemingly unending pause as my friend appeared as overcome by emotion as Dr Gentili had been. Finally Holmes asked as though in a trance "And what did you find in this trove of Vivaldi manuscripts?"

"Music without measure. Concerti and sonatas for all manner of instruments – violin, bassoon, violoncello, oboe, flute – playing as a soloist and in every conceivable combination – secular vocal music, sacred vocal music, operas – we did not even know he had written any vocal music or operas."

"Do you have any examples of the music with you?"

Dr Gentili reverentially drew a manuscript out of his brief case and handed it to Holmes. Even though I am no musician, one look at the torrent of notes poured out over the staves took me back twenty years to the moment when Holmes had first introduced me to the unbridled exuberance of Vivaldi's music.

Holmes took his violin out of its case. Was it the dust from the autograph, or was it a well of feelings that I had never before seen tapped that had made his eyes go bright? When he started to play from the manuscript, the notes came out in a bewitching stream of melody. The incomplete Brandenburg case had been one of the last cases on which I had collaborated with Holmes before my second marriage. The piece, of which Holmes now gave the first performance for perhaps two hundred years, took me back to the time of my wooing.

When he finished, Gentili and I sat in awed silence. It was Holmes who spoke first.

"I note this piece has a title – L'amoroso or 'The Lover'."

"Yes," replied Gentili, after a long pause as he in turn came to from the reverie into which we had all sunk. "Many of Vivaldi's pieces bear the name of a dedicatee – Morzin, who was Josef Haydn's first patron, or Bancardi, for whom he wrote a bassoon concerto – or they have descriptive names. There are four concerti named after the seasons, two different ones for flute and for bassoon called The Night and two different ones for violin and for flute called The Storm at Sea. But there are hundreds of pieces without name or title that are of equal merit."

"So may I ask, Doctor Gentili, why you wish to speak to me? You have made a musical discovery of unsurpassed value on which I congratulate you from the bottom of my heart. Surely the only question is how to progress to the academic study and publication of this treasure trove?"

For answer, Gentili turned over the manuscript of the concerto from which Holmes had just played an extract. Even with my untrained eyes, I could see that the last movement was incomplete. The piece simply broke off in the middle of a phrase.

Holmes looked stunned. He took out a magnifying glass and examined the binding that held the manuscript together.

"The rest of the music has been ripped off and the torso of the concerto roughly bound with other works. By the looks of the glue in the binding, this took place about forty years ago," he said soberly. "This is indeed a grave loss."

"In fact, in fact," assented Gentili. "In each bundle of manuscripts, the first item starts halfway through a movement and the last item breaks off before the end of a movement. The piece you have just played is the last item in a bundle."

"And what is your explanation for that?"

"Each bundle is marked with a letter of the alphabet: A, C, E, G and so on. That suggests to me that a larger collection was divided in half at some point and that what we have here is only one half of the complete collection of Vivaldi's manuscripts. This means there must be a parallel collection of manuscripts of equal size and quality waiting to be discovered, assuming it has not already been discovered, or been destroyed in the years since the binding took place."

Such was the momentous nature of Dr Gentili's deduction that it took a few seconds for its full import to sink in, even to Holmes. But when it did so, I had never in all my long years of collaboration with my colleague seen him so excited. "We must strain every sinew to find it!" he cried. "We have an opportunity here that will make the world of music ring!"

There was another pause before Holmes asked.

"Who else knows about your discovery?"

"I have told no one. From the beginning, my concern about these manuscripts was that someone else would come to hear of my find, would acquire the autographs and sell them among private collectors, which is the way to maximise the return on their sale. This would be a danger whether the discovery were made by another historian, or by a government official: my country's government is keen to sell national assets to finance its weapon-building programme. It would be a tragedy for scholars of music not to have all the manuscripts in one place where they can be studied together and where we can obtain an understanding of Vivaldi's working methods. I want to protect all these manuscripts in the National Library of Turin. And that is why I am here in London. I am an expert in musical style and structure. Tracing manuscripts, looking at watermarks and delving in archives is not my métier. Would finding the remaining autograph manuscripts be a commission you would like to accept? If you would undertake this commission, I would ensure that your name appeared as the inceptor of this project although I could not promise you a financial reward."

"My work, I have often said before, is its own reward and never has this remark been more apposite than now. Watson, our next stop is Venice and it is indeed a fortunate coincidence that you have the tickets already booked."

Before I could say anything, Dr Gentili said, "I knew you and your friend would not fail me."

When Dr Gentili had taken his leave, I turned to Holmes who had already lapsed into a world of his own as he studied the autograph that Dr Gentili had left us. "Holmes, how in the name of all that's wonderful, do you think I can get my wife to accept your proposal?"

"You have already said that your trip to Venice is something she knows nothing about," replied Holmes absent-mindedly as he was already absorbed in analysing the Vivaldi manuscript. "Tell her you have a chance to change the course of history, and I am sure she will regard your brief absence as a sacrifice worth making."

The next morning found Holmes and me on the boat-train from Victoria and the morning after that, we were crossing the lagoon to Venice. Holmes was as indefatigable as ever and we were soon in front of Dr Corso, head of the Venetian city archives. Holmes asked if he could see the wills and any other documents of members of the Vivaldi family.

My friend's name always carries instant recognition. All extant documents were soon brought to us and a clerk was placed at our disposal. We were reassured when it appeared that the number of documents was large, but less so when the clerk said that there was no will extant from Antonio Vivaldi. My friend sat down and went through what there was. His knowledge of opera meant that Holmes spoke quite serviceable Italian, which had already been of use to us in the case of "The Red Circle". Almost immediately, I saw a look of excitement as he looked through the will of Vivaldi's brother, Francesco, and found a receipt in respect of a payment for "Concerti ed altri brani da mio fratello, Antonio" from a Venetian senator, Jacopo Soranzo.

"Now we need to find documents relating to Senator Soranzo," commented Holmes. As the clerk took back the Vivaldi documents, he stamped the folder that contained them to show the date that they had last been accessed. Holmes looked to see the sequence of stamps and noted that while there were none in the thirty years before, the documents had been accessed for review only four months previously.

We reviewed files relating to Senator Soranzo and found a reference to a sale of music to a Count Giacomo Durazzo. Once again, the file had been taken out only four months previously and never before for many years.

"Someone else is evidently on the trail," said Holmes, concern etched deep on his features.

There were no personal or family documents on the Durazzo family in the archive, but a review of an Italian encyclopaedia revealed that Giacomo Durazzo had been the Venetian ambassador to Vienna in the mid-eighteenth century, where he had been a patron of the operatic composer, Gluck.

"Venice, Vienna, music. Our chain is almost complete!" exclaimed Holmes. "All we need to do is track down the descendants of Giacomo Durazzo. But I fear that there is every reason to think that someone else has got there first, that Count Durazzo's family vault will be empty of manuscripts and that his collection of Vivaldi autographs, such as it is, will already have been broken up and sold to collectors. Reassembling it will be like reassembling a shattered stained-glass window."

The Durazzos turned out still to be a wealthy family based in Genoa with only one surviving member who could be in possession of the documents. Further research showed that the current Count Durazzo was one of two brothers whose father had died in the 1890s. Holmes speculated that it might have been then that the collection of manuscripts had been divided between the brothers in the rough way referred to above, and that the monks had obtained their half of the manuscripts on the death of the other brother. Holmes sent a letter to the surviving Count Durazzo, asking to meet him. As we were under tight time constraints, Holmes wrote in the letter that we would travel to Genoa and asked that the modern-day Count Durazzo send a letter to the main post office in Genoa to await collection.

Immediately after posting the letter, we crossed Italy and stayed the night at the Hotel Astoria in Genoa. We waited impatiently in our hotel, going every few hours to the post office to see whether a response had been received. After two days, we received a letter from Count Durazzo, saying that he would meet us and inviting us to his house at half past ten the next morning.

With the diplomatic background of the Durazzo family, it was unsurprising to find that the austere-looking nobleman before us spoke faultless English. Holmes explained that our mission was to look at the Count's manuscript collection. The Count sat staring at us for several seconds before saying "I am, of course, aware of your name, Mr Holmes, and of that of your friend, but I must advise that you are not the first person to have asked me recently about autograph manuscripts in the vaults of my family."

"And," asked Holmes in a voice which conveyed little hope, "are these manuscripts still in your possession?"

"The man who asked me about them was called Gentili." I was about to turn to Holmes to ask him whether he could explain Dr Gentili's behaviour when Durazzo continued. "Gentili is a Jew and I do not treat with Jews. You and your friend, however, are free to search my family vaults. I have no interest in anything you might find."

I could see my friend hesitate as he thought how to respond to this outrageous statement, but in the end we were taken to the vault by a manservant of the Count, where we found the autograph manuscripts intact.

We parted company from Count Durazzo, promising to revert to him, and headed to Turin.

I could see that even Holmes was bewildered by our switchback ride between hope and despair, and he was silent as we sat on the train. We had telegrammed Dr Gentili to tell him of our impending arrival. He was on the platform in Turin waiting for us as our train drew in and took us to his home.

He congratulated us on our discovery and set about explaining his extraordinary actions. "When Count Durazzo refused to see me, I had to find someone whom he would be prepared to see. Mr Holmes, your name is like no other for opening doors. I could not tell you that I had followed the trail of the manuscripts from Venice to Genoa as you would not have been convincing as the discoverers of that trail if you had merely heard of it through me. It is rather like the way you, Mr Holmes, withheld the fact from Dr Watson here that you had survived the fight with Professor

Moriarty at the Reichenbach Falls, to ensure that his reporting of "The Final Problem" carried complete conviction of your death."

"Dr Gentili," said Holmes, with the rare smile he gave when he recognised a figure of comparable calibre to himself. "You did yourself an injustice when you said forensic investigation of music was not your métier. On the contrary, you have great perseverance and psychological insight. These qualities, combined with your knowledge of music, mean that you will rise high in your profession as a music historian. You might even consider criminal detective work as an attractive sideline."

"I trust that at least some of your prophecy will come to fruition," said Gentili, with a faint smile, although he did not explain precisely what he meant by this remark.

After a pause, Holmes said "We must now see how we can fund an appropriate buyer for the purchase of the remaining manuscripts."

"That too is being arranged," said Gentili. "I have had contacts with two public-spirited local industrialists, Signore Foà and Signore Giordano. Tragically, both men had sons who died in infancy and they are between them prepared to put up the money to buy the manuscripts to commemorate their sons. They want to have the music published with pictures of their infant sons on the front cover. The publication will be called the Mauro Foà and Renzo Giordano Edition."

In spite of his apparent indifference, long and complex were the negotiations that followed with Count Durazzo, so it was not until 1930 that the complete set of manuscripts could be brought together. The works, almost all in autograph, comprised eighty secular cantatas, forty-two sacred works, twenty operas, one oratorio and no fewer than three hundred and seven instrumental pieces.

Holmes and I travelled out to Turin to be in the library to see the crowning of Dr Gentili's work as the bundles of manuscripts arrived from Genoa.

The date was set for the afternoon of 30 June and by special permission Holmes and I had a chance to examine the new manuscripts on the morning. Holmes had brought his violin and opened one of the bundles from the Durazzo collection. He eagerly plunged in a hand and pulled out the autograph of a violin concerto. He was just about to play from the score when I heard him say "How strange!"

The autograph of the concerto bore a dedication at the top: "Per i Brandenburghesi" ("For the Brandenburgers"). Holmes put down his bow to look more carefully. "Well!" he said eventually, as he drew himself up, "This is a violin concerto which Vivaldi has written for the court of Brandenburg. The solo part is designed for him and the fairly simple string parts are for the customary four-part ensemble. How strange that there was no sign that Vivaldi had worked at the court of Brandenburg when I examined the archives there. I shall have to give this matter some thought."

That afternoon, when the announcement of the acquisition of the trove of Vivaldi manuscripts was made, Holmes and I were front-row guests. We had expected Dr Gentili to make the speech to mark the announcement and were very surprised to learn from a library official that Dr Gentili was indisposed. The speech to mark the occasion, we were further surprised to discover, was not given by any of the academic or library representatives but by the Prefect of Turin, who wore a military uniform. My Italian was not of a level to understand what he said, but I noted that he repeatedly used phrases like "eroe Italiano" and "il mare nostro". Holmes meanwhile was cast deep in thought and was only awoken from his reflections when at the end, the assembled gathering broke into a stirring song which I learnt afterwards was called "Giovinezza, giovinezza, primavera di bellezza". I could work out that this meant "Youth, youth, springtime of beauty." I also knew that Vivaldi had written a concerto about spring, but the melody to which the words were set sounded of an altogether different era and the line "Fascismo è la salvezza della nostra libertà" seemed quite out of place.

The next day we went to Gentili's house and knocked on his door. After a considerable time, and only after he had fully satisfied himself as to our identity, and that we were unaccompanied, he let us in.

"I am afraid," he said, "that as a Jew I have to keep a low profile if a government official is present. Accordingly, I stayed away from the festivities yesterday. My professional activities are being increasingly circumscribed by the actions of my government."

Holmes raised the matter of the concerto Vivaldi had written for the court of Brandenburg. "Vivaldi had benefactors and patrons across Europe for whom he wrote concerti," said Gentili. "It is new to me, but it does not surprise me that he wrote for the court of Brandenburg. If the string parts were simple, it is possible that he will have also used it for the girls' school in Venice at which he worked for many years. He will then have been able to claim a fee for the same work twice over."

Holmes turned to me. "You will recall, Watson, that I had to discontinue my investigation into the circumstances behind the composition of Bach's Brandenburg concerti. With this discovery, I wonder whether it is worth re-opening the investigation and claiming the balance of the reward." He turned back to Gentili and asked him "Would you be interested in travelling to Brandenburg and investigating Vivaldi's activities there? I would be happy to commission you with this work for, in your investigative skills, I feel a talent akin to my own."

Gentili flushed with pleasure at Holmes's words and accepted the invitation with alacrity. "If the results of your trip to Brandenburg did not accord with your expectations," he commented, "it is perhaps because you did not know where to look." Once again Dr Gentili did not explain his words.

Holmes and I returned to England. Within a few days, Holmes was back at my door, having arranged another meeting with Dr Gentili. The Italian looked excited after his trip where, backed by a letter from Holmes, asking for access to the Brandenburg archives, he had spent a week amongst the shelves.

"Vivaldi," said Gentili, "was often known by his nickname of the Red Priest or Il prete rosso. So sometimes, in my searches for his manuscripts in other archives, I have found them filed under the name Rossi. Looking in the Brandenburg court archives for documents under that name I found a letter in Vivaldi's hand to Johann Sebastian Bach where he tells Bach of a large orchestra in Brandenburg, with outstanding trumpet, keyboard and violin players as well as a patron with a taste for unusual sonorities and musical structures. I found nothing in the payroll records in the archives to substantiate Vivaldi's claim of the scale and complexity of the ensemble, so I can only conclude that Vivaldi wrote the letter to send Bach on a false trail. When Bach submitted a group of his own concerti that were unplayable by the ensemble in Brandenburg, it was a guaranteed way of making sure that no commissions from Brandenburg ever went to the German master. And that would leave the field open for Vivaldi."

"Do you have the letter?" asked Holmes.

"Unfortunately, I was not authorised to take the original but I have transcribed its contents here. Vivaldi wrote it in Italian and the court translator made a German version to send to Bach, which is why a copy of private correspondence between the composers was retained in the archives. From what I have seen, Bach was completely taken in by Vivaldi's ruse. I also found evidence of several payments to Vivaldi in respect of his works although they were paid under the name Rossi. Vivaldi thus had both the means and the motive to deceive the great Bach and he seems to have made the most of the opportunity."

As my reader will be only too aware, the 1930s was a time of gathering storm clouds in Europe. Holmes submitted Gentili's findings to the Bach Society, who were dismayed to find out how Vivaldi had made a fool out of their hero and declined to give the findings, which they received under Holmes's name, any publicity at all. They nevertheless gave Holmes the reward due to him for fulfilling their commission, though whether this was to fulfil the contract, or to attempt to avoid publicity, I would not speculate. The condition for payment – that Holmes should not disclose the discovery to anyone – suggests the latter. In any case, Holmes passed the reward he received to Gentili in such a way that the Italian authorities would not hear of it.

At the time of writing, in early 1950, and after the end of the Second German War, it seems right to bring the story of Vivaldi, Bach and the Vivaldi autographs up to date.

The Brandenburg archives were destroyed in a bombing raid in late 1944, so no original of the letter Gentili discovered there will ever be found.

Gentili returned to Italy after his last trip to London and was barred from working at the University of Turin. He endured difficult years before and during the war. After the conflagration was over, he wrote to Holmes again to thank him for the munificent reward from the Bach Society that had made surviving the war years slightly less difficult. He is now working on cataloguing the vast collection of music in Turin and remains engaged in making new discoveries of works by the great Italian master. Publication of the manuscripts has started with pictures of the two infant boys, Mauro Foà and Renzo Giordano, on the front.

And although Vivaldi himself appears not always to have shone in his dealings with patrons, employees and other musicians, this does not of course detract from the beauty and vitality of his music. In next year's Festival of Britain, a week of concerts has been planned dedicated to it. The pieces to be played – which provide a good selection of his instrumental works – have been advertised as being the first modern public performances of Vivaldi's music, although I feel privileged to recall that I heard the first modern private performances of two of the pieces many years ago when they were played by Mr Sherlock Holmes.

A Seasonal Tale

My reader will need no reminding of the extreme cold of the early months of 1895. The winter of 1894/1895 brought only two cases to add to my annals – one in late December 1894, immediately preceding the advent of polar conditions across the country, and one that came our way at the end of March 1895 just as the last frosts were clearing. Holmes was able to resolve neither case to his full satisfaction, but both threw up similar, profoundly existential questions of a type Holmes and I never explored at any other time. Furthermore, these two cases occurred next to one another in the list of cases we investigated and, although their main events took place several months apart, they reached their conclusion within minutes of each other. Accordingly, it makes sense to treat both under one narrative.

The 25th of December 1894 dawned gloomily. Holmes looked out of our window onto the street below and then up at the sky as it at last became light just after breakfast.

"That the Romans felt the need at this time of year for a celebration of *Sol Invictus*, the unconquered sun, should not surprise us," he commented sombrely. "The Stygian darkness in these last days of December is all but unending, and the human desire to seek a pattern in events that are either random or beyond our control almost irresistible. On our first acquaintance, good doctor, I said to you that I get a bit in the dumps sometimes but that I soon get right. This unending dreariness allied to an absence of any stimulating work is just the sort of thing to precipitate such a mood and it is but a paltry comfort that the winter solstice is now behind us."

The sky was indeed a leaden grey and, as I pointed out to Holmes, although he gave no sign that he had heard my remark, the most colourful thing to be seen from our window was the dun brickwork of the buildings opposite us. It was soon after this exchange that, to my great relief, our sitting room played host to a new petitioner, although the man who interrupted our gloomy observations was the most down-at-heel client we had ever received. Holmes had previously remarked that his most interesting cases tended to come from the needier classes of society, but when I looked at the ragged and aged figure in front of us on that early morning, I confess that I had the lowliest expectations.

"My name is Michael," he said after much prevarication and obfuscation, which I abbreviate for the sake of clarity, "and I am a groom at the stables of the great lunatic asylum in St George's Fields in Southwark. There have been some very strange goings-on over the last two days and I thought I should discuss them with someone, but I had no idea who the right person might be. There is a very big stable at the hospital, but it is largely for the use of visitors coming to see their sick relatives. So a groom always needs to be present as the hospital has visitors at all hours of the day or night and our doctors work some strange hours. I normally work through the night to make sure that all is well."

"Pray continue," said my friend leaning forwards in his chair. I could see from his expression that he was keenly interested by what our visitor was saying, even though I could not see where this exposition of our petitioner's problem was taking us.

"Last night I came into work at nine and found a woman and a man in our stable. They had appeared from nowhere – the groom I had relieved had made no mention of them. Working in the sort of place I work in, you're used to seeing some strange things, but this was new to me. The couple said that they had been on a long journey, had nowhere to stay and had decided to put up in our stables. She was heavily pregnant and, to my complete astonishment, said she proposed to give birth where she found herself. I called on my superior to explain my problem, but he said there was no room for anyone in the hospital and suggested I saw what I could do to make the man useful. So I set him to repair some of the mangers which needed fixing, and it was obviously something he had done before as he made a right good go of it."

My reader will understand that Michael's apparent claim that the nativity story was happening in his stable had already caused me to dismiss him as a harmless prankster, but I could tell from Holmes's alert poise and bright eyes that he was fully engaged in Michael's narrative.

"Just after midnight last night," continued Michael, "the woman – though, in truth, she wasn't much more than a lass of thirteen or fourteen – gave birth to a baby boy whom she laid in one of the mangers which her husband had repaired while I upped and came here."

"Anything else?"

"Well, I was hoping you would supply the 'anything else', Mr Holmes. A woman giving birth in my stable would be trying enough for anyone."

Holmes thought for a moment. "Are the couple and their baby still there?"

"They are, sir."

"Then we must go to the stable now and speak to them. These events you describe from St George's Field are indeed so out of the ordinary as to require an investigation."

I was uncertain of whether to accompany Holmes on what seemed to me to be a wild-goose chase on a day when the consumption of the fatted goose at midday was what was uppermost in my mind. He turned to me, however, and said, "Watson, none of the events you have ever written about have been as worthy of your pen as these in Southwark. I would beseech you to join us."

Faced with an imprecation such as this, I had little choice but to follow. At my friend's insistence we got into two cabs, although I noticed the driver of the one that took Holmes and Michael was very reluctant to accept a fare as shabby as the groom. Holmes had to insist he wanted our petitioner with him in the cab.

It was mid-morning when we arrived in Southwark and I was surprised as we walked from the cab to the stables to hear the sound of wonderful music floating through the air. I was for a second at a loss as to where the beautiful tones were coming from until Holmes provided an explanation:

"Many asylums," he commented breezily, "employ talented musicians to organise their music. You will remember, Watson, the rather unusual case of a few months ago when the West Country musician, Edward Elgar, consulted me on creating a musical riddle. Elgar directed music at the main lunatic asylum in Worcester and I have no doubt a musician of similar calibre is directing the music we can hear now."

The full exposition of Edward Elgar's consultation with Holmes may form part of a future narrative, but among Holmes's suggestions to Elgar was that the latter did not need actually to create a musical riddle at all – he merely needed to state that his music contained one and the public would create a mystery and possible solutions for themselves. Holmes further advised that the application of a mystery, however spurious, to the work would increase its marketability. The well-known Enigma Variations was the product of this petition to Holmes by Elgar.

"Yes sir," said the groom, seemingly impressed by Holmes's surmise. "The asylum's musicians have been practising since dawn for their next concert. It seems a strange time to do it, but, as I said to you, strange things happen at strange times in this place."

We went into the stable, which had none of the odours I would normally associate with such a place. Instead there seemed to be a hint of incense in the air. The couple that Michael had told us about were sitting in the stable in a pool of light cast by a beam of watery December sunshine which shone through a hole in the roof.

"Good morning," said Holmes. "I am Sherlock Holmes and this is my colleague, Dr Watson. We came to see if you needed any help. Can the medical assistance of Dr Watson be of service to you?"

The wraith-like girl of whom the groom had spoken really was only about fourteen. She had dark eyes which peered at us from olive skin, and she held us in a steady gaze before she said, "I have slipped the surly bonds of Earth. Sunward I've climbed, then swooped in tumbling mirth. I have danced the skies on laughter-silvered wings of sun-split clouds, and done a myriad things. And there, where neither lark nor even eagle ever soared, 'tis there that I have consorted with my Lord."

The fire, the poetry and the complexity of her statement quite took my breath away and, when I glanced across at Holmes, I saw a look of wonder cross his face too. The girl's voice was of the utmost serenity and fitted with the glorious streams of music we could hear from the orchestra and choir practice. But the accent was uneducated and, when I saw this young girl seated in these humblest of surroundings, I felt like looking round to check, in case the words had come from the mouth of someone else.

The man, who had similarly dark features, came forwards.

"What are we to do?" he asked plaintively in the same rough accent as the girl. "My fiancée has kept making these weird remarks ever since she fell pregnant and I don't understand them. I thought the place to take her was an asylum, where there might be someone who would understand her, but they would not make room for her and said we should stay in the stable ... I don't know what to do."

After some further discussions, I performed a brief medical examination of both the woman and the baby and established that their condition was normal in every way.

I turned to Holmes and said, "I don't know what there is for us to do."

Holmes said, "We must seek some proper medical care for the mother. A stable is no place for someone who has just given birth, and there is clearly more to be worried about than just her physical condition. Come with me, Watson, and we will see whether we can at least get this lady a bed here for a couple of nights."

It was only on the walk from the stable to the hospital building that I was able to articulate the thoughts which had first stolen into my brain at Michael's initial and confused deposition, but which were now pounded through my head like a peal of bells.

"Holmes!" I exclaimed. "This truly *is* the Christmas story. There are too many similarities for it not to be!"

Holmes turned to me with his finger raised to his lips. "As we saw in the case of Jonas Oldacre which you describe in 'The Norwood Builder', a detective should always seek an alternative to the obvious explanation. I shall investigate this mystery as I would any other."

To my relief, the senior medical officer in the ladies' ward of the hospital was the good Dr Bridge, a man I knew as my old tutor on brain fever from my days as a medical student. He expressed astonishment that anyone heavily pregnant, especially someone making delusional remarks, would have been turned away at the door of the asylum. "We do what we can here to help anyone in need," he said, "and an extreme case such as you describe, Watson, would certainly be offered help."

He agreed to take the couple and their baby in for at least three nights, and Holmes and I returned to the stable to bring them the good news.

When we got there, to our consternation, not only had the couple and their baby gone, but Michael had disappeared and his successor as the duty groom was a man who knew nothing about any couple who had been staying in the stable. It is almost certainly irrelevant to the narrative that I now tell, but the music had stopped, while the doors and windows had been thrown open so that there was no trace of the heady perfumes which had wafted round the stalls only a short time previously.

The much younger man who had come on shift was curt and unhelpful. No, Michael had not briefed him of anything special at the shift change. He had spent his time since he came into work cleaning up the mess that had been left by what he regarded as Michael's neglect of his duties. The new groom had done such a thorough job of this that even on close examination by Holmes, there were no signs of any couple having spent the night in the stable.

There seemed nothing more to do, so Holmes and I once again got into a hansom to take us back to Baker Street.

My friend was silent, but I could see puzzlement writ on his face, and he scanned passers-by as we drove north-west as though in the hope he might spot the couple and their baby. He maintained his silence for the rest of the day, but charged and recharged his pipe with the strongest tobacco. I was just about to take my candle to bed when he unbent himself.

“It doesn’t make sense, Watson: that the couple took fright and disappeared before we could help them is unfortunate but not impossible; that Michael left as soon as his shift came to an end is unhelpful but not unreasonable; but where did that girl learn to speak like that? It was uplifting, but wholly inexplicable. It is almost as if some other force had taken over her body because she won’t have learnt to use words like ‘myriad’ and ‘consorted’ in any schooling that she will have had.”

“So what are you going to do?” I asked.

“I shall have to see what I can do to track the couple down. I shall not stint in my efforts to trace them. This mystery must be investigated like any other matter, especially if what we are investigating should prove to overturn the received version of events of two thousand years ago.”

For the next few days, Holmes was seldom at our quarters. He told me afterwards how he called at inns and lodging-houses, spoke to beadles in work-houses, deployed the forces of the Baker Street Irregulars, and consulted with the police about missing persons’ lists. He found no trace of any missing couple and a child. It was as if the people we had seen had disappeared off the face of the earth.

And it was not long before he had to abandon the search altogether. After that mildest of Decembers, January started with a succession of bitter frosts, with the glass showing temperatures well below freezing point for days on end. I spent almost all of the next two and a half months indoors, swathed in blankets. I had sold my medical practice and Holmes had no cases apart from the abortive one referred to above. Our fellow Londoners also preferred to stay indoors as far as they could and the normally busy thoroughfare below us was empty indeed.

The extreme cold meant that coal could not be moved, so our rooms in Baker Street became icy and cheerless as our stocks of solid fuel dwindled. Our solitary gas ring, which we kept burning all day, became our only source of heat. The Thames froze over and, on those infrequent days when newspapers could actually be printed and distributed, they carried reports of numerous deaths from exposure, hypothermia and sheer inanition. This prolonged spell of extreme cold lasted throughout January and February and well into March.

Holmes occasionally remarked querulously that the London felon was a dull fellow not to take advantage of the absence of people and the frozen conditions to settle a few scores. But I noted that he was as disinclined as I was to leave the relative warmth of our quarters for the rigours of the snowy wastes outside. His intellectual energies, by contrast, were unaffected by the cold and he channelled these energies in a most unexpected way in his search for the couple and their baby. The year 1894 had seen the small matter come to pass that I have related under the title "The Crooked Man". To resolve the case, Holmes had shown a knowledge of the Bible which had quite taken me aback as I was not aware of any interest on his part in sacred texts. Now, as we sat on either side of our flickering gas ring, my friend engrossed himself in Bible study, minutely examining both the scripture itself and exegeses of it. It might be anticipated that over such a long period of close confinement, Holmes and I might have had conversations ranging over a wide range of subjects, but Holmes's biblical study occupied him fully and we exchanged barely a word with each other.

It was late March – after a long thaw had chased away the last frost flowers from our windows while the first buds were visible on the trees – before my friend provided an exposition of his work. "What say you," he asked one bright though still bracing morning, "to a ramble though Regent's Park?"

It was not in Holmes's nature to propose a walk for the sake of it and I ascribed his uncharacteristic suggestion to a lack of detective activity allied to a desire to escape our frowsy living room. I happily assented to the invitation.

For a couple of hours, we strolled together – though always staying on marked paths or on the Outer Circle as the grassed areas were quagmires now that the thaw had set in. We found ourselves by no means alone in our perambulation as other Londoners fled the warmth of their hearths to enjoy the fresh air. On the Outer Circle we saw pedestrians, cyclists and carriages, as well as a few intrepid motor cars, each, in accordance with the law of the time, following a man bearing a red flag who was obliged to walk at the maximum permitted speed in towns of two miles per hour. These cars regularly blocked the path of the swifter, horse-drawn two-wheelers and four-wheelers.

I asked Holmes about the case at Southwark and whether he had any plans to pursue it further.

"I fear," he said, "that if you come to make any account of it at all, you will probably have to treat it as one of those unfinished cases which you have elsewhere referred to as being often not the least interesting of the numerous matters that are brought to my attention. You will recall that the couple and their story bore many similarities to the nativity. Having been unable to continue my missing persons search in the midst of the bleak winter, I have focused my intellectual energies on Bible prophecies and associated writings."

"And are your conclusions from these that the baby we saw represented the Second Coming of Christ and that the end of days is upon us?"

"I think not," said Holmes in a voice shorn of much of its normal assurance, "or I would have told you the story of the giant rat of Sumatra. The ending of days would have justified its publication whether the world was prepared for it or not."

This was not the first time Holmes had mentioned the giant rat of Sumatra without telling me why the world was not yet prepared for the events associated with it. I hoped that he would elaborate on his statement, but instead he continued to talk about the case from December.

"The New Testament has an altogether apocalyptic vision of the Second Coming, which is said to be preceded by great famines and wars, with the sun darkened and the moon not giving light. For all the prolonged harshness of the recent winter, there are no phenomena of such magnitude identifiable at present. No, the events we saw have far more characteristics of the prophecies of the first coming of Christ. Most of the predictions of a first coming were in the writings of Isaiah, and the Gospel of St Matthew draws heavily on Isaiah to authenticate the birth in the stable as the birth of the son of God. Isaiah states that a child will be born of what is variously translated as a virgin or a young woman, although my understanding of Hebrew is that Isaiah was referring to the latter. Matthew, by contrast, states unequivocally that the mother of the person he describes as the Redeemer was a virgin."

"As you will understand Holmes," I said, reddening slightly at the thought, "I would not have been able to form a view on this point after the woman we saw in the stable had given birth. My limited examination could only confirm that she was about fourteen and in good health for someone who had had a recent confinement."

Holmes paused as though to docket the information I had just given him and then continued, "Another prophet, Micah, says that the Redeemer will be born in Bethlehem while Hosea states he will come out of Egypt."

"But, Holmes, this baby was born in London!"

The long fallow period in my friend's caseload had not diminished his acerbity with those who he perceived as intellectually slower than himself. "The asylum, Watson, is called Bedlam as it was originally founded at the priory of St Mary of Bethlehem. Accordingly, the birth we saw agrees precisely with Micah's prophecy."

"Holmes!" I exclaimed, although in retrospect I may have been imprudent to raise my voice, "If what you are saying is that the birth in Southwark was the Coming of the Redeemer, you are overturning the teachings of the Christian church of almost two millennia. In less benign times than these, you might have been burnt as a heretic, just as your powers of deduction might have had you burnt as a witch!"

"Precisely for this reason I have been most circumspect in talking to you about the results of my enquiries. Not only did the couple in the stable satisfy many of the requirements of the original prophecies, but I can find no way to explain how the girl might have learnt to speak in the way that she did."

"So what are your plans now?"

"The matter is certainly a most engaging one – but my efforts to locate the couple had borne no fruit even before the advent of extreme cold, and the trail now will be even harder to follow after the long hiatus in the investigation imposed by the weather. Although I will carry on some further researches for as long as my practice remains quiet, I fear the Southwark case will remain unsolved and the question of whether the birth overturns our current version of history will remain unresolved for many years to come."

When we returned to Baker Street, the boy in buttons was waiting for us. "A gentleman called, sir! He said he will be back."

No sooner had we gone up the stairs than our client appeared in the doorway.

In my story "The Minister and the Moguls", I introduced the slight, inscrutable Mr Lawler who always came wearing an opera hat. At the opening of that story, he had been a junior member of the British Cabinet. The story ended not only with the result Mr Lawler had sought for his political party, but also with further profit for him in the form of a new and highly remunerative non-executive directorship at one of Britain' s leading companies, for which he resigned his Cabinet post. Holmes and I could not be sure if either of these things were the result of our efforts and I had assumed that we would not hear from Mr Lawler again. I was therefore surprised when Mr Lawler appeared once more at our threshold. He was as elegant and cordial as he had been at the time of the original case and, after the customary formalities, he came straight to the point.

"I am a busy man, Mr Holmes," he said as he lit a cigarette. "In addition to my assiduous work as my constituents' proud representative in the House of Commons, and my onerous responsibilities as a non-executive director supervising the activities of some of Britain's biggest businesses, I also represent a number of non-governmental organisations. One of these is the organisation behind that well-known annual publication, *The Climate Almanac*. This well-funded group watches the weather and the climate closely. We at *The Climate Almanac* are convinced that the climate is changing. We have had a succession of hard winters culminating in the icy horror that we have just experienced and this seems to form a pattern with the succession of poor summers over the last few years."

Mr Lawler was about to continue the exposition of his problem, but I had seen puzzlement spread across Holmes's face from the start of Mr Lawler's statement. Even though it was clear that Mr Lawler had much more to say, my friend could restrain himself no longer.

"My dear Mr Lawler," he interjected. "I have attempted in my own small way to be a benefactor of humanity, but I am at a loss to see how I can help you in this matter. I cannot, even with all the powers that my chronicler, with occasional embellishment," and here Holmes nodded in my direction, "attributes to me, in any way influence the weather or alter the climate."

"Just so, Mr Holmes, just so. A commission asking you to change the climate is not the motivation for my visit." I think Mr Lawler expected Holmes to interject again, but my friend remained silent. Lawler continued. "A few years ago, some construction workers building the Metropolitan Railway came upon some enormous boulders that were blocking the path of their tunnel by Finchley Road station."

I saw Holmes raise his eyebrows at this seemingly irrelevant piece of information.

"Mr Holmes," said Lawler, accelerating his flow of speech, I suspect in fear that Holmes was about to terminate the interview, "the rocks were of such a size and density that they could not be dug out and were so massed in the soil that it was impossible to tunnel round them. In the end they had to be dynamited out. Scientists at the geology department of University College in London had expressed an interest in the rocks and asked if they could examine the fragments that were subsequently extracted. It is only in the last few weeks they have arrived at their findings and presented an early draft of them to us at the *Almanac*."

"And?" said Holmes.

"Mr Holmes, the rocks were all that was left of a gigantic glacier."

For the first time since Mr Lawler's arrival, I saw a spark of interest appear in my companion's eyes, but he let Mr Lawler continue without interruption.

"Glaciers normally end in a deposit of rubble, but this conglomeration of rocks was the tip of no ordinary glacier," said Mr Lawler. "This glacier had extended to the north from where the station was being constructed as far as we can measure. This means that at some point in the distant past, the ice sheet which covers the North Pole and which at present ends thousands of miles to the north of us in the inhospitable wilds of northern Norway, must have extended to cover almost the entire area of this country. The recent prevalence of harsh winters has caused us at *The Climate Almanac* to ask ourselves two questions: first, whether such bitterly cold times are poised to return and secondly, if there is anything that mankind is doing to bring about this change. Without wishing to labour the obvious, the weather comes from the sky and the last hundred years have seen an unprecedented increase in the amount of coal and other fuels being burnt as part of the process of industrialisation. This means that far more soot, brimstone and associated gases are being released into the atmosphere than has been the case at any time in the history of mankind. Could the increased presence of these gases be blocking the light of the sun and so causing a cooling of the climate for all that such gases are invisible to the human eye?"

"Pray continue."

"I have had the opportunity to discuss my concerns with the Prime Minister. He agrees with me that the matters I have raised are a danger not only to the fortunes of those who live in this country but to the well-being of everyone on this planet. He is reluctant to invest government money directly behind an idea which may prove to be no more than the wildest speculation. Our organisation, besides what it receives from its benefactors, receives grants from the Government. These grants are to be increased in the next financial year as the Government would like more information from us on tides and currents to assist with the optimal operational efficiency of the Royal Navy. This will free up funding to enable us to widen the scope of our activities. *The Climate Almanac* would like to commission you to find out what you can about meteorological history and to establish whether the recent swing we have seen towards colder winters and cooler summers has anything to do with man's activity."

I glanced across at my friend to gauge what he thought of this commission, which was quite unique in all the petitions for his help that I had heard. He was, however, inscrutability itself and merely told Lawler that he would have to consider how to respond to his invitation to investigate climate change and man's role in it.

Mr Lawler expressed delight at Holmes's words and, with a flourish, produced a cheque book and a receipts book with the name of *The Climate Almanac* embossed on its front to document the payment of an advance to Holmes to the sum of £100. "Naturally, Mr Holmes," he said, "it is only fair to make an advance of the consideration you will receive for taking on this case."

I think Holmes was slightly surprised at the receipt of such a munificent advance when he had yet definitively to accept the case. Nevertheless, he picked up the cheque given to him by Lawler and tucked it into an inner pocket. Forthwith, Mr Lawler was gone as suddenly as he had come.

I challenged Holmes once we were alone again. How, I asked, could he accept an advance for taking on a case when he had not even formally agreed to carry out the investigation? How, I went on, did he propose to investigate changes in the climate over a period that was long enough to be scientifically meaningful, and how was he going to establish whether the great industrial revolution of the past hundred years was influencing the climate? And had he finally decided to abandon the case that had come our way just before the freeze?

Without answering, Holmes sat back in his armchair with his eyelids drawn three-quarters of the way over his eyes and the tips of his fingers pressed against each other. There was a long silence before he finally spoke. When he did so, his voice had a strangely disembodied quality:

"The newspapers have been full of stories of the poverty caused by the prolonged cold weather. For all of the industrial developments that Mr Lawler has spoken about, the economy remains largely agricultural. If the weather makes farming impossible, farm labourers cannot work, yet they must still eat and pay their rent. Equally, the long freeze has made my own flow of clients dry up, while my expenditure has remained at the same level or even higher due to my need to pay for my share of the gas to keep this room warm. I do not enjoy an army pension or the benefit of capital derived from the sale of a medical practice. And my research into the couple we saw in the stables at Bedlam has not only proved completely fruitless, it is also, even if I continue with it, not going to give me any income. However much I dislike having my priorities swayed by financial considerations, a commission from a well-funded organisation such as that behind *The Climate Almanac* is most welcome to me at the present time."

"But surely any future payment from the publishers of *The Climate Almanac* and any further payments for a project of this nature are dependent on you confirming a link between the cooling of the climate and industrial development? Are you really willing to countenance such a meretricious *modus operandi*?"

I saw Holmes start at the mere suggestion that his funding might be dependent on the conclusions that he arrived at rather than on his decision to accept a commission. A lengthy silence ensued as he considered his position.

"I am fully seized of the professional requirement to retain my independence and integrity," he said at length. "Nothing will persuade me to abuse the powers with which I have been endowed to give a false opinion. I shall conduct my research and pronounce my opinion on my findings without fear or favour even if the answer I give is not to the liking of *The Climate Almanac*."

"How do you propose to investigate a subject as complex as a possible change in the climate?" I pressed. "For your own activities, you have me, with all the inadequacies you regularly point out, to act as your chronicler. The climate does not enjoy the services of any similar biographer whom you can consult."

"On the contrary, dear Watson," said Holmes, unbending slightly. "There are few topics which have attracted greater volumes of ink over the centuries. From Homer talking of rosy-fingered dawn three thousand years ago, to the records of monks in the Middle Ages, and the writings of otherwise under-employed country parsons over the last two hundred years, we are blessed with weather reporting that, while lapidary in nature, is nothing if not comprehensive."

For the next two weeks I again saw little of my friend. He was gone before I breakfasted and I had retired by the time he returned. On one occasion I caught sight of him when I visited the London Library in St James's Square. He sat surrounded by printed papers and yellowed manuscripts. But though his eyes turned in my direction, he bore a glazed expression on his countenance, and was far too engrossed even to acknowledge me.

One evening he returned to Baker Street and warmed himself by the fire for a few minutes before nestling into his customary armchair. He sat back, filled his pipe and lit up.

"I am not a man easily given to fear, Watson," he said at length, "but I have had three very near escapes today. Although the Southwark case might have proved dangerous to me, my complete failure to track down the couple in the stable means that I would not expect any assault from anyone espousing the current view of Christian history. Other than that, my casebook remains as empty as ever, while the investigation I am undertaking on the climate seems to me to be a mere sinecure for an overfunded non-governmental organisation."

He paused as he recharged his pipe, tamping down the tobacco before he spoke again.

"Crossing Cavendish Street this morning, a two-horse van whizzed out of a side street and was on me like a flash. I sprang for the footpath and saved myself by the merest fraction of a second.

The van dashed round by Marylebone Lane and was gone in an instant. The whole thing happened so quickly that I was unable even to see any identifying feature on the vehicle, but I continued my journey with extreme wariness thereafter. On Oxford Street, a solitary rider apparently lost control of his mount, which reared up onto the pavement and knocked me off my feet. It was only by reacting the instant I struck the ground that I was able to avoid being trampled underfoot. The horse, its rider grappling with the reins, galloped off round the corner, but to have had two near misses in the space of a couple of minutes was disconcerting in the extreme. Such a sequence of events has only occurred to me in the final stages of my struggle with Professor Moriarty and, were I not entirely satisfied that he lies at the bottom of the Reichenbach Falls, I would suspect his malign influence in this."

"Did you not raise these apparent assaults with the police?"

"I had nothing of a sufficiently tangible nature to convince them. They attributed the assaults to the animals being hard for their handlers to control after their long idleness. The officers I spoke to said that they had had a spate of such incidents reported to them. This does not explain the third brush with death I had."

"A third brush with death? That must surely rule out the possibility of coincidence."

"I decided to return from the London Library to here via a circuitous route. As I was boarding an Underground train at

Embankment Station, I felt something like a push in the back and almost ended up on the rails. I turned round, but could not identify who my assailant might have been in the heaving crowd."

"So do you think these apparent assaults are a consequence of your research into climate change or revenge for previous brushes with the criminal world?"

Holmes did not answer but drew his violin to his chin and, unusually for him, played a soothing melody which I did not recognise. This continued for several minutes before he put the violin back into its case.

"Moriarty's gang is gone," he said eventually. "There is no criminal currently on the loose capable of launching a campaign of terror against me. The Bedlam case is inactive. The only case I am pursuing is into weather patterns and that field of research is the preserve of harmless eccentrics and the otherwise under-occupied – not of dangerous criminals."

"So what is your next move to be?"

"We head out of London tomorrow."

"Out of London? To where?" I ejaculated.

But Holmes would not say. Instead he leant down to tend the fire and then stood again before it, although for the first time for several months our sitting room was not cold. Although I reiterated my question, he would not be drawn further and eventually I retired to my room.

The next day we descended the stairs of the house in Baker Street and proceeded with great circumspection south towards the Metropolitan line station at the junction with the Marylebone Road. I had packed an overnight bag. To my surprise Holmes had not only an overnight bag but also something that looked like a weighty tool box. A couple of hansoms trotted past us and when a third offered its services to us, Holmes sprang into the road to hail it and then dragged me inside. He barked at the driver, "Victoria Station as fast as you can go!"

On our journey down to Victoria Station, Holmes regularly leant out of the window to check that we were not being followed and leapt to his feet in alarm when the cab went over a section of the road that had been potholed as a result of the recent frosts. He sat down with a brief apology, but even at the time of "The Final Problem" I do not think I had seen him so obviously on edge.

At Victoria Station he booked us two tickets to Pulborough. It was only when we were seated in our compartment in the first-class carriage of the train that was to take us to Horsham on the first leg of our journey that he relaxed a little and, puffing at a cigar, started to adumbrate on the findings he had made from his research into climate history:

"At the time of the compilation of the Domesday Survey in the late eleventh century, vineyards were recorded in forty-six places in southern England. By the time King Henry VIII ascended the throne, the climate had improved to the extent that there were one hundred and thirty-nine sizeable vineyards in England and Wales and our towns are full of road names such as Vine Street and public houses called The Bunch of Grapes. There are now no longer any commercial vineyards in this country and all wine is imported."

"But Holmes," I countered, "could the decline of English vineyards not just be due to the fact that the wine they produced was not very good and the vines not particularly productive? I would suggest that increased prosperity and improved means of transport mean that it is cheaper to import grapes than to grow them domestically."

"That may be admissible, but consider this: there were no frost fairs on the Thames until 1606. This period of colder weather seems to have started in the early seventeenth century. There were seven frost fairs on the Thames starting in 1607 with the last one eighty years ago in 1815."

"But you are merely pointing out seven extreme winters in a period of over two hundred years, the last of which was nearly a century ago. You cannot base any firm conclusions on anecdote and a few isolated observations."

"A very astute remark, dear Watson, and that is why we are heading into Sussex. You will remember the case I told you about, which began my professional career as a consulting detective even before I first knew you. You will recall that I lived in Montague Street by the British Museum and had very few cases. You produced a version of this, the first case that brought me to the wider attention of the public – "The Musgrave Ritual" – where I saw that what seemed to be a nonsense rhyme was in fact a set of instructions identifying a historical treasure's location."

"But why are we visiting a scene of a long-closed case of yours to look into developments in the climate?"

"You will recall that two trees – one an elm that had probably been three hundred years old when it was struck by lightning ten years before the case, and one an oak which is over a thousand years old – played a significant role in the story. I propose to look at the growth rings of the trees to see what I can make of changes in the climate over the last thousand years."

"How will you look at tree rings of the oak tree unless the tree is cut down?"

"I have this tool box with me containing a large drill. I hope the remains of the elm will provide me with sufficient information to avoid having to drill into the trunk of the great oak – it was twenty-three feet in girth last time I saw it – to look at the rings in it. But just in case this proves to be necessary, I have already telegraphed my old acquaintance, Reginald Musgrave of Hurlstone House, to obtain his permission to do this."

After an uneventful journey, we arrived at Hurlstone House. My reader may have seen pictures or read descriptions of the famous old building – the oldest in the county – and its splendid landscapes, designed like so many parks in Sussex by that renowned park planner, Howard Lucie.

Musgrave, a slim, debonair figure the same age as Holmes, was at the threshold of the great house to greet us. "Pleased to meet you, Dr Watson!" he commented amiably. "I note from your retelling of Holmes's previous investigation down here that our fellow student Hugh Trevor, you and I are the only people who call him Holmes rather than Mr Holmes, or sir. I read too, Holmes," he continued, turning to my friend, "that your brother calls you Sherlock – strange that I should never have known your first name. I must say I take great pride that Hurlstone House, uniquely among the settings of your adventures, should feature twice. I have got some of the gardening staff readied in case you need any help."

We went into the park and first of all looked at the stump of the great elm. It had been cut right down but Holmes spent a considerable amount of time with a hand lathe smoothing out the surface. Musgrave told us that the elm had been struck by lightning in 1870. Holmes counted the rings. There were three hundred and forty of them, meaning that the tree had been growing from 1530. I could see Holmes was on a hot scent, as his eyes were bright and his tone brisk.

"Look at this tiny ring," he exclaimed at one point. "This is the year 1816, the year famously without a summer – and almost no growth in the tree." He carried on with his minute examination and in the end sat up and lit his pipe. "This tree stump undoubtedly offers evidence," he said. "The rings are noticeably narrower after 1607, meaning that the tree enjoyed better growth conditions in the years before then. But our data from here only extends back another sixty-seven years which is too short to draw any conclusion. We will have to drill into the oak tree."

The core of the ancient oak proved almost adamantine, especially as Musgrave was insistent that no permanent or visible damage should be done to the tree. Nevertheless, the drill had eventually driven a hole a substantial distance into the wood. Holmes reached into the depths of his toolbox and pulled out, to my considerable surprise, an instrument which I recognised as an endoscope. That he should even have heard of such a specialist medical instrument spoke volumes for the breadth of his learning. More time passed as he called out to Musgrave and me, acting as his scribes, what he could make out while he peered down the tube. We took notes of what he said.

"This year confirms what the elm told us about 1666 – a hot summer – and here we are back in the late sixteenth century … Most of the tree's growth seems to have been before then as we are only a quarter of the way in ... warmer summers in the sixteenth century and earlier, coinciding with the growth of English viticulture, and again between 1450 and 1480."

Eventually he rested from his endeavours and sat down with us.

"I have seldom come upon an investigation with such a complete record of data, for all that this is the first time I have sought to construct a case of this type," he said as he lit a cigarette. "There is a clear reduction in the width of the tree rings after 1550, suggesting a cooling of the climate and a deterioration in growing conditions. That coincides with the decline of vineyards after the reign of Henry VIII, poor harvests prevalent at the end of the reign of Queen Elizabeth I and the start of frost fairs in London in 1607."

"So there is a cooling of the climate!" I exclaimed.

"We progress," said Holmes, "but we have only covered half the ground. You remember that we were commissioned to establish not only whether there was a deterioration of the climate, but also whether this was due to industrialisation. This cooling precedes what is known as the industrial revolution by several hundred years so we are halfway to ruling out industrialisation as a cause of the recent cooling of the atmosphere. We must, however, check whether industrialisation is accelerating this cooling. We are at present only at the halfway point in our investigations."

We set off back to London and Holmes outlined his next steps in the train. My friend was much more relaxed on our journey home though whether it was due to his progress in establishing an unbroken narrative of climate history dating back several hundred years, or to the absence of any further apparent attacks on him I could not be sure. In any event, there were no worried looks over his shoulder or stratagems to put a would-be pursuer off his track.

"We are indeed touching on some old history in this case, my friend," he enthused, as our train headed north, "looking back into the fifteenth century, looking in at Reginald Musgrave's and, for our next step, returning to the great hospital at St Bartholomew's, where you and I first met. We must conduct some experiments on the heating and cooling of objects in a bell jar to see what effect the changing of gases in the atmosphere has on the way the objects warm and cool. St Bartholomew's hospital is the only place which would be able to provide me with the equipment for such an experiment."

We spent the next day in the laboratory where, with my assistance, he carried out numerous experiments along the lines he had proposed. At the end of the day we sat down next to each other on laboratory stools and he explained his findings.

"My experiment has produced a rather unexpected result," he confided as he drew on a cigarette. "My measurements established a time for how quickly objects warm and cool when heat is applied to them in a bell jar. I then added increasing quantities of first dioxide of sulphur and then dioxide of carbon to the air. The dioxide of sulphur seemed to have no effect on the speed with which the contents of the bell jar changed temperature. The dioxide of carbon, on the other hand, resulted in a slightly lower rate of cooling although I have not yet devised a theory of why this should be. Could the dioxide of carbon hold in heat released by the earth but at the same time let heat transmitted to the earth by the sun pass through?"

"So what are you going to say to Mr Lawler? That is not a conclusion that corresponds with his view of climate change."

"As I indicated to you, Watson, *magna est veritas et praevalebit* – great is truth and mighty above all things. I shall not allow what I say to be swayed by pecuniary reward and shall tell Mr Lawler my conclusions as I see them. I will set them out in a report. I will qualify my findings, which only cover a few hundred years and stress that, while I have observed the apparent warming effect of carbon dioxide on the atmosphere, I cannot explain it."

Holmes wrote a note to Mr Lawler and an appointment was agreed at Baker Street at ten o'clock on the following day.

Just before the appointed hour, the buttons knocked on the door and presented, to my own surprise and that of Holmes, the couple whom we had seen in the stable with their by now fourteen-week-old baby. Their son, a bonny lad with a shock of blond hair and clear blue eyes, made a sharp contrast to the couple's dark features. The girl was fully engrossed in looking after the baby and it was the man who did the talking.

"I wanted to thank you, Mr Holmes, for your attempts to help us in January, even though we chose not to take you up on it," he said. "After you left us in the stable, it suddenly occurred to me where I could get help for ourselves. We are of nomadic stock and there is a small place in Buckinghamshire where such people gather. We got there before the cold set in and have been there ever since."

"Indeed," said Holmes calmly although I could see that he was still puzzled. "I confess I conducted a thorough search for you, and I would be grateful if you could disclose to me where in Buckinghamshire that was so that I can close a gap in my network of contacts."

"It's just north of Slough, sir. You wouldn't have heard of it but it's a hamlet called Egypt because lots of gypsies gather there."

"Ah," said Holmes, "I shall indeed have to broaden my network of people I retain to look out for me." Holmes looked even more discomfited after this disclosure but his voice was bland as he added. "I am glad that matters have resolved themselves. I confess, it is not my normal practice to involve myself in intimate family matters, but may I ask if your fiancée is still saying things that trouble you?"

"I've learnt to get used to it when she says things that sound a bit funny," replied the man. He looked lovingly down at the child in his fiancée's arms. "I wonder how he will turn out."

The couple went almost as suddenly as they had come and before Holmes or I could make any further comment, Mr Lawler appeared at our door, as full of smiles as ever.

"So, Mr Holmes," he said, "have you been able to establish a cooling trend in the climate? And is industrialisation a contributory factor?"

"My research," replied Holmes calmly, "supports the view of a cooling in the climate compared to the Middle Ages, starting in the last quarter of the sixteenth century and continuing until today. I cannot speculate that this will intensify or reduce in the future, merely that we are in a colder epoch than the period leading up until the end of the reign of Queen Elizabeth, although it is, obviously, warmer than the period when the glacier remnants were deposited at Finchley Road station."

"That is very clear," said Mr Lawler, and puffed at the cigarette he had lit on his arrival. "And is this change man-made?"

"I have dedicated time to this matter also and I have two reasons for saying that man's activity is not the cause, although more research may find it is a contributory factor. First of all, the cooling of the climate preceded industrialisation by about two hundred years. Secondly, my research on increasing the level of carbon dioxide content in air suggests that such a process has a warming rather than a cooling effect on the climate, although I cannot explain the reason why. I have written a fuller report in this file here," said Holmes, picking up the dossier he had prepared, "which presents these findings but cav—" I could see that Holmes wanted to continue with the qualifications to his conclusions, but Mr Lawler had heard enough.

"That is excellent! Excellent!" exclaimed Mr Lawler, full of enthusiasm. "Your findings are clear and logical and, indeed, confirm researches I have been conducting elsewhere." With a flourish he again produced his cheque book and wrote another cheque. "I think we'll say another £900 to make it a round £1,000. It is good to have one of the great minds in the country working on a project of this importance, Mr Holmes. Your name is a *sine qua non* for convincing those in high places. And thank you, as ever, for your help too, Dr Watson," he added, bowing to me.

Within an instant he was gone, and only the presence of the cheque betrayed he had been in our sitting room at all. The dossier Holmes had prepared lay on an occasional table.

"So what do you make of the events of this morning?" Holmes asked me.

"I do not know what to think," I commented. "We have seen two cases resolved as far as we are concerned within a few minutes of each other and in both cases our clients departed as precipitately as if they had never been here."

Holmes himself disappeared shortly afterwards. When he returned, he explained, rather contrary to his normally opaque practice, that he had gone to the bank to deposit his cheque. For the rest of the day he sat smoking in his chair and said not a word.

It was only when I got the newspapers the next day that matters started to fall into place. They were full of the newly discovered threat of climate change with many commentators ascribing the threat to the rapid industrialisation of the last one hundred years.

By contrast, *The Daily Telegraph* carried a different angle. Here, a spokesman described as being close to the Prime Minister was quoted as saying, "The Government is not of the view that recent industrialisation is the cause of climate change. Our evidence suggests that it is a cyclical event which started long before the process of industrialisation. This is confirmed by research carried out by Government scientists, which has received independent endorsement from the great Baker Street detective, Mr Sherlock Holmes. This research suggests that the burning of coal and other petro-chemicals and the consequent increase of carbon dioxide in the air actually has a mild, warming effect on the atmosphere. Accordingly, it is proposed that the Red Flag Law be abolished to encourage the use of vehicles powered by internal combustion engines."

The Motor Car Manufacturers' Association responded to the news with the statement: "We welcome the proposed abolition of the Red Flag Law as long overdue. We have long argued that the speed restrictions on motor vehicles are unwarranted and, as it is now clear that relaxation of such restrictions may temper the natural cooling of the climate, the abolition of the so-called Red Flag Law is a sensible measure to take. We are grateful to the Government's scientists and to Mr Sherlock Holmes for their assistance in establishing the truth about climate change and its causation. London is indeed fortunate to have some of the age's great minds at its disposal for such research." The spokesman to whom this statement was attributed was Mr Lawler.

"But neither the Government nor Mr Lawler has included any of the qualifications that I made to the opinion," said Holmes, looking perplexed. He was going to continue when the buttons knocked on the door, bringing in a registered letter. When Holmes opened it, he found it was an enquiry from Buckingham Palace, asking whether he wanted to be considered for inclusion in Her Majesty's Birthday Honours list.

My reader will recall that after our last encounter with Mr Lawler, Holmes had a mental collapse which had left him slumped in his chair, chain-smoking through the night. I was anxious to avoid a recurrence of this and thought the best way of doing so was to ask him about his next steps on the Bedlam case. To my surprise, however, he was far more anxious to talk about our work for the organisation behind *The Climate Almanac*.

"The climate change case is a good illustration of the dangers of having a small amount of knowledge. My research has only gone back about four hundred years, but the Government has chosen to use it to suit its own preferred theory and to make major policy decisions based on it. It is clear that the climate is fully capable of massive change irrespective of any human activity – otherwise we would not have remnants of glaciers at Finchley Road which must date back to a time when this country was almost uninhabitable. It is also unclear what effect a big increase in the emissions of carbon dioxide and other gases may have on the climate over a period of several hundred years."

"So what are you going to do now?"

"There is nothing I can do now about how the Government chooses to use my research. I will have to regard this as a valuable lesson in exercising caution in my dealings with the Government. In future, I shall be most reluctant to be associated with short-term decisions based on data I regard as inadequate."

"But I note you banked the cheque."

"I banked the cheque because I had completed my assignment. I had prepared a full report which expressed a clear view though with qualifications and it was Mr Lawler who chose to seize on the one part of it which suited his objectives," said Holmes, although he sounded a little defensive.

There was a pause and, most unusually, it was Holmes who seemed anxious to fill it. Lighting a cigarette, he continued.

"The idea that glaciers may once have covered this country is an intriguing one and I will have to do more research on it. I propose to travel into the northern wastes this summer to monitor the movements of the glaciers there. Mr Lawler's cheque will give me the means to do so."

This trip was subsequently mentioned at the end of the matter I have chronicled under the title "Black Peter". I was surprised, when the story was published, that Holmes's proposal of a trip to Norway did not attract more attention from my friend's followers, for it was a complete *non sequitur* to what had gone before and was only included to explain the dearth of cases from the summer of 1895.

To hold Holmes's attention, I pressed him about the assaults he had faced in London on the day before we had gone to Hurlstone.

"With the case behind me, I am inclined, as the police suggested, to ascribe them to animals becoming hard to control after a long period cooped up, rather than to any human agency."

"But that is surely an illogical reaction," I countered.

I noticed Holmes, for the only time in our acquaintance, twitch nervously at the unprecedented suggestion from me that he might have behaved illogically.

"At the time of your investigation," I continued, "you thought that the climate change case you were working on was the preserve of harmless eccentrics and yet you thought there was a plot to assassinate you. In fact, the construction that is being placed on your work will lead to the wiping out of the livelihoods of many people working with horses as the use of motor cars becomes more widespread. Such people – if they had become aware that your work may lead to this – would have had every motive to wish you ill. Yet now when we find there was a real motive to do you harm, you dismiss the notion that you were in danger and attribute two potentially lethal assaults on you to natural causes. And the assault at Embankment Station had a purely human agency. In fact, your investigations both into the climate change and the nativity would have given cause for many people with vested interests to want to be rid of you."

"I suspect, Watson," said Holmes after some thought, "that I may have become over-suggestible to random events for the same reason that the animals – which seemed at the time to be under the control of forces I could not identify, so as to carry out a concerted assault on me – may have become over-exuberant."

I thought that Holmes was going to terminate our discussions after this and dreaded what his next action might be. Instead, after several further puffs on his cigarette, he sat up, focused his eyes into the distance and continued speaking in a manner that suggested he was still fully engaged.

“The two recent cases have much in common even though their outcomes are so different.”

“I had not observed any commonalities, other than the fact that their time spans seem to have overlapped.”

“Ah, still the same old Watson, able to note and record events, but unable to see the full canvas.”

I think Holmes was waiting for me to interject, but I waited for him to continue.

“Surely,” he finally went on, “all the cases of mine you have so far been good enough to chronicle have been concerned with identifying ‘facts’ – a word derived from the Latin *factum*, the perfect participle of the verb ‘to do’. Here, the focus of our investigations has been on predicting the future and any inferences we may make will never be uncontested. Meanwhile, people always try to fit facts to suit their theory. This is clearly the case in the climate change matter and is also the case in the births at Bethlehem and at Bedlam.”

“Perhaps you could expand on your theory?”

“The main biblical predictions of the birth of a saviour were that he would be born in Bethlehem and be born to an ‘almah’, which is variously translated from the Hebrew as ‘a young woman of marriageable age’ and as ‘a woman who has not known a man’. You saw how easy it was to fulfil the requirement regarding place of birth here in London, just as the requirement that a child be born of a woman of marriageable age is easy to comply with. And the virginity of either the Bethlehem mother or the Bedlam mother is impossible to disprove, as you yourself, a qualified doctor, would attest. You will note that subsequent events also confirmed Hosea’s prophecy of an Egyptian provenance for the child. Satisfying the biblical prophecies whether here or in what we call the Holy Land is not particularly difficult and the couple with their child did precisely that.”

There was a long pause. In the end I myself broke it by asking Holmes, “And what is the commonality with the climate change case?”

“We were able to find facts to confirm a narrative. We had a theory postulating a pattern of declining temperatures and found evidence to confirm it, even though investigation over a longer period might have shown that it was the cooling of the climate that was aberrant to the longer-term trend, or that cooling was a longer-term trend. Mr Lawler has used the trend for his own purposes to bring about a change in the law. In the same way, it is easy to seize on the Bethlehem birth as meeting the Old Testament prophecies with the consequence that we have had a Christian church for almost two thousand years, although the Bedlam birth fulfils the prophecies just as well."

"And which case, if either, do you personally believe to have been of long-term significance?"

Holmes thought for a moment, opened his mouth as though to say something and then closed it again. Finally, he shrugged before saying, "I fear what you ask me is not part of my remit. My trade is in the elucidation of events in the past, rather than the prediction of what will be believed in the future. Even after nearly two millennia, people are still disputing the significance of the birth in Bethlehem. Thus I cannot even resort to evading your question by saying that time will in the end be the arbiter of the matters we are discussing. In both cases, indeed in all three cases, we are on the border of what we know and what we believe. I fear that eliminating doubt in matters such as these is beyond even my powers."

A Dutch Sandwich

One day in late 1907, just after my second wedding, my wife and I were sitting over breakfast when the maid came in with what she described as an urgent message. I had gone back into practice at our newly established home in Queen Square and picked up the envelope with some anxiety as only a serious medical case would normally bring a note meriting such a description. It was with a mixture of relief and joy that I recognised Holmes's characteristic small neat lettering on the envelope. The message inside was terse:

"Must see you about softwear case. Come to Baker Street for quarter to ten this morning."

"What is 'softwear'?" I asked my new wife when the maid had left the room.

"Really, John," she replied with a shy smile and perhaps the merest hint of a blush. "You appear to see but not to observe." She paused to take a sip of tea.

My new wife had a wonderful skill in taking me back to my prime years in Baker Street and, as she paused for breath, I wondered where her explanation of what softwear is would take us.

"If you still don't know what softwear is, we will, dear John," she continued serenely, "have to undertake some more clothes shopping together." As well as being adept in selecting a clever turn of phrase, my wife was a devotee of London's choicest fashion outlets and this was not the first time she had used an apparently unrelated topic as a segue into a suggestion of a further purchase of items of clothing. "For us ladies," she murmured with eye-lashes fluttering alluringly, "softwear is the very latest thing. The current trend in ladies' clothing is for dress that is figure hugging and so it often contains embedded within the cloth so-called stiffeners such as whalebone or thin pieces of cane to hold it in place next to the body. Softwear is a brand of clothing manufactured by the London Softwear Company. The products are imported from the Low Countries and are subject to a special finishing process in London which is, I understand, of Dutch origin."

"Do you know anything about this special process?" I asked, my curiosity piqued.

"I do not. The process is described in the Company's advertising material as being special and secret. The outcome of it is, however, that their outfits are of the most stylish appearance with the same fine cut offered by other clothing designers, but they offer the wearer considerably enhanced levels of personal comfort. Accordingly, the clothes command a significant premium to those of London Softwear's competitors. You have often been with me when we have bought Softwear products, but the details of our purchase have obviously escaped you. It is clear we must plan another shopping expedition at the earliest moment to give you a full opportunity to see and observe my buying habits."

My bank balance was still at a parlous level as a result of the triple set of costs arising from our recent wedding, the fitting out of the new living quarters and the purchase of a medical practice whose opening days had been notable for the absence of patients. Accordingly, I feigned deafness at my wife's remarks and, glancing at the clock, commented "Half past eight already. By the time I have completed my toilet, found someone to take on the practice for the day, and got to Baker Street, it will already be close to the appointed hour."

"You are right, my darling," said my good lady. "You go and sort out your case with Mr Holmes. I know the resolution of his problems is a source of great joy to you. I trust you will return from your labours with a happier demeanour and, perhaps, the willingness to accompany me on a round of purchases to avail ourselves of the latest product offerings from that great couturier, the London Softwear Company."

Within a few minutes, I had washed and shaved, had arranged for the nearest practice to take on my few patients for the day, and was walking to King's Cross Station to take the Metropolitan Line to Baker Street.

Holmes was as austere as ever in his welcome when I arrived and set to immediately in briefing me on what he knew of the case:

"You will remember Mr Lawler. He is by now a Member of Parliament of long standing and this is another in a series of cases associated with him which bear a distinct political slant. Previously he has brought to our attention matters involving climate change and the tobacco industry. The cases have never been less than stimulating and this one promises to be no different. He has written to me asking advice on a matter involving a business, London Softwear, which is based in his constituency. I have no detailed idea of what softwear is, although I understand it appertains to a female's intimate apparel. I was rather hoping that with your greater exposure to the habits of the distaff side, you might be able to provide some additional insights."

I told Holmes what my wife had told me and he listened attentively. "Your comment that this finishing process is of Dutch origin naturally tells me all I need to know about it," was all he said when I had come to the end of the explanation given by my wife. I was somewhat crest-fallen by my seeming inability to tell Holmes something that he did not know already, but my curiosity was nevertheless piqued for a second time in the space of two hours.

Holmes, however, would not be drawn into any further discussion of the London Softwear finishing process and continued

"Incidentally, it is not only I who wanted your insights on this case. Mr Lawler, by some chance, seems to have become aware that you are no longer resident here in Baker Street and specifically asked that you be present at our interview this morning if possible. And here is the man himself to explain matters to us."

Even though I had previously met Mr Lawler several times before, I had never ceased to be amazed by his manner. He seemed to materialise out of thin air in the space framed by the lintel, jambs and threshold. His face was as ever wreathed in smiles.

"My dear Mr Holmes, how excellent to see you again! And the good Dr Watson! A delight that you are here too. I am bound to say I was not sure I would have the pleasure of seeing you here as I had learnt you have moved out of Baker Street to become a constituent of mine. This is why I asked Mr Holmes to ask you to come as I am aware of the great services you have performed in the matters on which I have previously petitioned Mr Holmes."

I had not yet taken any steps to discover who the Member of Parliament was for my Queen Square residence, but Mr Lawler was only too happy to explain. "I have the honour to be the Member for Bloomsbury and Clerkenwell, so Queen Square falls within my constituency. Normally, dear Dr Watson, it is my duty to serve you as your elected representative in Parliament, but in this case it is your services and those of Mr Holmes of which I wish to avail myself."

"Perhaps you would like to expand on what you wrote to me last night, Mr Lawler?" asked Holmes.

"The London Softwear Company is much the largest employer in my constituency. They have a technique of finishing garments which are shipped in from Amsterdam. This process enables the garments to meet the modern taste in fashion while affording the wearer considerably ameliorated levels of personal comfort. An employee at the factory came to my constituency office yesterday and informed me of rumours that this finishing work in the London factory will be moved to Amsterdam. The closure will be a disaster for my constituents. The jobs at the factory are highly skilled and well rewarded by the standards of our times. Thus for every job at the factory that goes, two additional jobs within my constituency will disappear as ancillary suppliers to the London Softwear Company are put out of business."

"You make yourself very clear. And what is it you wish me to do?"

"I need you to infiltrate the London Softwear Company and establish whether the rumours are true and, assuming they are, to find out if there is any way to prevail upon the London Softwear Company to change its mind. In my position as a Member of Parliament I am unable to offer you any pecuniary reward for this service, but I am sure that Dr Watson will see, as a doctor serving the needs of his patients, that it is in his interests to ensure that the finishing of ladies' garments in Bloomsbury continues."

"Very well," said Holmes. "There is obviously no time to lose. The cause is an excellent one, which I would seek to pursue irrespective of any financial considerations."

When Mr Lawler had gone, I turned to Holmes: "How do you think a man trying to establish a medical practice has the time to engage in industrial espionage?"

"My dear doctor, how do you think a man trying to establish a medical practice can afford to permit the precipitate pauperisation of his potential pool of patients? I have already established that the London Softwear Company is in Southampton Row. I suggest we go there immediately. You can present yourself as what you are – a newly established practitioner anxious to offer your services as the company doctor – and you can present me as your assistant."

Within the hour we were at the London Softwear Company's Southampton Row premises. Its imposing building was just south of Russell Square. We walked through an archway into a courtyard, at the centre of which stood an elaborate fountain with a myriad cascades and rivulets. Above the water, rainbows appeared and evanesced in some welcome late-autumn sunshine. A section of the courtyard where carriages would normally be parked was cordoned off, but this was no obstacle to us as we had taken the

Metropolitan line from Baker Street and had walked from Euston Square. We presented ourselves at the reception and, in no time at all, were in the office of Mr Scott Alleyne, a man who bore the grandiose title of Global Head of People.

Mr Alleyne was a tall man with oiled black hair and a hearty manner. "A company doctor is just the sort of thing we are looking for," he said when I presented my credentials, "and we always look favourably on people with a military background. We employ two thousand people on this site and they are our greatest asset. Accordingly, their safety and well-being is our primary concern. Having a company doctor whose practice is only a few hundred yards from our door is exactly what we need to show our commitment to our workforce. Next Thursday, we have a surprise for our employees. We will gather all of them together to mark five years of the London Softwear Company when we shall celebrate not only the success of the company but also the numerous good works we do through our charitable foundation, which our Managing Director actively supports."

Mr Alleyne paused to give us a slim but lavishly illustrated booklet on the company's welfare activities, which I looked at briefly before I passed it to my assistant.

"I shall take the opportunity to make an announcement of your appointment to the workforce and I would be grateful if you could be present for this. I would take you in to see our Managing

Director now, but he is in Amsterdam today and will not return before next Tuesday. I will arrange a meeting for you with him in due course."

Within a few minutes we were back on the Southampton Row.

"Well," I commented to Holmes, "no sign there of imminent closure."

"My dear Watson," said Holmes. "Are you really telling me you failed to see the obvious signs of imminent closure at the London Softwear Company's premises?"

"I saw none at all. He expressed his commitment to his workforce and is already making plans for their future."

"So here we are in late November 1907 and yet there was still no 1908 diary on his desk."

"But Holmes, not everyone is as adept as you are in planning their appointments ahead."

"Did the cordoning-off of part of the courtyard not strike you as strange?"

"Doubtless it was to enable some minor repair work to the façade of the building to be carried out unimpeded."

“It is far more likely it was to enable a security firm to be able to establish itself quickly on the day of the announcement of the closure and to protect the company’s assets, not to mention its senior management, from the violent wrath of the terminated employees.”

“You make the space cordoned off sound like a parking spot for the four horsemen of the Apocalypse!” I quipped, though Holmes’s observations were already starting to undermine my confidence in the long-term future of the factory in Bloomsbury. “And in any case, why do they want to employ a Company Doctor if they are going to announce the closure of the site?” I asked, though even I could detect a slightly faint tone in my own voice.

“If a riot ensues on the announcement of closure, they will doubtless want medical staff on hand to deal with any people suffering from injuries.”

“But Mr Alleyne even took an interest in my military background.”

“I assume he wanted a doctor with a military background because such a practitioner will be used to treating open wounds and to carrying out rapid and drastic surgery,” replied Holmes. I suspect my friend could see my increasingly wan expression and he pressed home his advantage. “Did you fail to observe the curriculum vitae Mr Alleyne had on the desk in front of him?" he added.

"Holmes," I retorted with some asperity, "I have had the honour to work with you for long enough. Whatever you and others may say, I have learnt to see and to observe. Mr Alleyne is the Global Head of People, so recruitment forms part of his brief. I was thus entirely unsurprised to see a document headed 'Curriculum Vitae' on his desk."

"But the curriculum vitae had Mr Alleyne's own name on it. While he may reckon on surviving any moving of production to another site, he is nevertheless making sure he has cover against the wind. Accordingly, he is in search of another position and this, along with the absence of a 1908 diary and the cordoned-off space in the courtyard, suggests that announcement of closure is imminent. I assume that it will be made next week when the entire workforce is gathered for what they think is the celebration of London Softwear's success. The coached-in security staff will be at the ready to prevent the workforce gathered in the courtyard from returning to the machinery on the factory floor to wreck it, or from launching physical attacks on the management when the announcement is made."

Even after more than twenty years of association with my friend, his capacity to leave me open-mouthed at his acuity and far-sightedness was undiminished. We walked in silence the few steps back to Queen Square where another demonstration of his ability to see, observe and infer was soon to follow. At my invitation he came in for a late lunch. "So very little structural work was required on your house when you moved in, I see," he commented, as we walked up the stairs to the front door.

"No indeed," I said, as I opened the front door. "The people who had this house before us invested heavily in the exterior – so heavily, in fact, that they were unable to meet the costs and fell out with each other. That was how we were able to afford it, as they were obliged to make a sale at a distressed price, although it did mean that the interior had been substantially neglected and this entailed significant expenditure on my part to rectify. I confess, Holmes, I cannot see how you spotted that."

"Structural work normally requires scaffolding which leaves behind scratches in the cement in the area," replied Holmes airily as he stood before the doorstep. "I see such scratches on the cement below, but with moss growing over them, which suggests that they are not recent. Thus the deduction was merely a somewhat facile demonstration of my art."

We sat down in our lounge and puffed at our pipes. I was comforted by the aroma of tobacco as Holmes's forebodings about the future of the London Softwear Company's premises in Bloomsbury filled me with gloom.

"So what are our next steps to be?" I eventually asked.

"The Managing Director is in Amsterdam. He is returning early next week and must do so through Victoria Station. I cannot believe a final decision has yet been made, so I shall find out what I can about him and track him on his return. Be you prepared to come to my aid at a moment's notice. Much hangs on this case – the livelihoods of many hundreds of people, not to mention a useful source of recurring income for a newly established medical practice in need of more patients."

I had not long to wait. On the following Tuesday, as foreshadowed, Holmes sent an urgent message asking me to meet him at twelve Bloomsbury Square. It was just getting dark when I got there and I looked around vainly for Holmes. Suddenly I heard a whisper in a familiar voice from a man driving a hansom: "Step in here, Watson! There is no time to lose."

I leapt in. As I did so, the heavy wrought-iron gates of number twelve swung open and a four-wheeler with a driver and a footman swept out and headed south.

My readers will be used to hearing colourful opinions on a wide range of subjects from their hansom cab driver, but may not always give their full attention to what the driver is saying. There was no danger of that happening here. Although our coach thundered along as it struggled to keep pace with the fleeter four-wheeler, I strained my ears to pick up what Holmes shouted to me from his driver's perch.

"The Managing Director of the London Softwear company is Mr Peter Velder," he yelled down as I pressed myself into my seat with my feet wedged to the floor and my hand clutching the armrest. "He arrived back in London this afternoon and was picked up by his coachman at Victoria Station off the boat-train. I have an arrangement with Mr Barlow, one of the Baker Street cab drivers, that I can use his cab when I need it for my own purposes. It has been of inestimable value to me as a means of pursuing cases where a carriage chase is involved."

The events I have described so far had seen my powers of observation traduced by both Holmes and my wife, but no great observational skills were required to assess that Holmes was highly talented at driving a hansom.

"I followed Mr Velder to his address, which you saw," continued Holmes. "As he got out of his coach to go into the house, I heard him shout to his driver that he would need the coach again in an hour. I am agog to find out where Mr Velder is now bound for."

"So what is my role in this?" I shouted up. "Surely your pursuit would be easier without me?"

"I will explain your role," came a reply I could barely hear over the clangourous rattling of the wheels, "at our destination," and Holmes fell silent.

I don't think I have gone as fast in a hansom cab as I did when Holmes was trying to keep up with the four-wheeler. We hurtled south onto New Oxford Street, down Charing Cross Road, around Trafalgar Square and into Whitehall. Mr Velder's coach turned right to go into Downing Street, but Holmes pulled in to come to a halt opposite the turning.

"I shall have to be swift," he said.

He returned a few minutes later. "I went to the telegraph office and sent a telegram to Barlow asking him to come here as soon as possible. I hope Mr Velder does not come out of Downing Street before Barlow arrives because part of my agreement with Mr Barlow is that I never leave his cab unattended."

"But Holmes!" I exclaimed. "When Barlow picks up the cab, we will have no means of swift pursuit when Mr Velder returns."

Holmes gave me no answer but instead hauled a bag out from under the driver's seat of the cab and pulled some clothing out. "Slip into the cab, Watson and change into these. I have had livery made up to replicate that of Mr Velder's stable staff. His coachman and footman are in for a surprise."

I quickly did as bid and soon Holmes was changed as well. A few minutes later a cabbie arrived.

"So what is our plan now?" I asked, looking mournfully first at the cab taking my normal clothing away and then down at the alien uniform I was wearing.

"We are here to look for …" Holmes paused as another cab drew up on the other side of Whitehall. "We are here to look for that!" he said and pointed theatrically across the street to where Mr Alleyne was getting out of the cab. His cab drove off and he walked into Downing Street.

"I reasoned," continued Holmes, "that Mr Velder was unlikely to take any action without consulting a third party. He was also unlikely to take any action without Mr Alleyne being kept fully informed. I knew I would not have time to infiltrate myself into the office of any third party, but I thought there was a fair chance Velder and Alleyne might get into a coach together and I would be able to listen to what they were saying."

"But how are we going to get close enough to do that?"

Holmes reached into his pocket and extracted two sealed bags, one of which he gave to me. "Inside the bag is a chloroform-soaked cloth. These cloths are to be our weapons. We will incapacitate Mr Velder's coaching staff, impersonate them with these uniforms and listen to what Mr Velder and Mr Alleyne discuss in the coach when they come out."

"But what will we do with the unconscious bodies?" I protested.

The passing of years had not made Holmes any less inclined to display his disbelief at my slow-wittedness. He stared at me before saying: "We are in Whitehall, dear Watson. The sight of a couple of apparent drunks lying slumped against a wall will occasion less surprise here, in sight of the Houses of Parliament, than anywhere else in the country."

We crossed Whitehall and went into Downing Street. Doubtless at some point in the future, Downing Street will be closed off to those without a permit, but our access to the street was unimpeded. With cat-like tread, we stole into Downing Street, crept up to the driver and the footman, and pounced! Within seconds they had joined other bodies slouched against one of the buildings of Whitehall. And an instant later my friend had taken his place in the driver's seat and I was sitting next to him.

And only just in time! Mr Velder and Mr Alleyne emerged from number eleven Downing Street shortly afterwards. We could see them pause in the doorway to shake hands with the familiar figure of the Chancellor of the Exchequer. I got down from my seat and opened the door of the coach, keeping my face out of the flickering lamplight. I overheard a last snatch of the conversation between the Chancellor and the board members of the London Softwear Company:

Mr Velder said “We would again stress the uniqueness of the process, and ask you to give our petition favourable consideration. The alternative to our proposal would be distressing indeed.”

Then the three men said their farewells.

“Let us go back to Bloomsbury for some dinner,” said Velder to Alleyne as the two men climbed into the coach. “We have something to celebrate! Driver, rather than taking me straight home, take us to the Royal Dutch Palace in Sicilian Avenue for some dinner.”

I noted that Holmes drove with great circumspection, which made the conversation between Velder and Alleyne easy to overhear above the sound of the moving carriage.

“That went much more easily than I anticipated,” said Velder. “I had planned to explain in detail about the special techniques of deep stitching applied to our garments in London. I was going to tell him that the technique had been devised in Amsterdam, so it was only right that a significant royalty should be paid there.”

“He didn’t even ask whether we had ever had any employees in the Netherlands,” chortled Alleyne.

“I told him that the goods were shipped from Amsterdam. I did not tell him they were made in Manchester and shipped to Amsterdam to give them the cachet of being imported. But, Mr Alleyne, that brass plate of London Softwear’s new holding company on the wall of our lawyers on the Herengracht will need regular polishing. As Global Head of People, maybe you should recruit someone special for the task.”

“If the Press finds out about our deal with the Chancellor, maybe we should offer the job to him.”

Both men laughed.

“So did our advisers tell you how much tax will we pay on London Softwear’s profits in the future once the Chancellor has given his final assent to our proposal?” asked Alleyne.

“I have always considered ‘nugatory’ a very useful word,” said Velder serenely. “No one has the least idea what it means.”

“But we will of course continue to employ two thousand people. And they will get improved health care. Maybe we should open another charitable foundation?” hazarded Alleyne.

“You can’t have too many of those. Good to have plenty of pictures of our charitable works in the company’s annual report. I’d rather the shareholders focused on our good works rather than on the directors' emoluments."

Both men laughed again and by this time we were in New Oxford Street. Shortly afterwards, we dropped our two passengers at the entrance to Sicilian Avenue which, unusually for a street in Central London, is pedestrianised.

"You can take the coach home, driver," Velder called up to us. "I shall walk back home from here and Mr Alleyne will take a cab to his house."

We drove the coach into twelve Bloomsbury Square, stabled the horses and returned to Queen Square. Then Holmes and I sat over cigars while he elucidated the discussions we had heard:

"The factory, it would appear, is safe. London Softwear are in the process of agreeing a special deal with the Chancellor whereby they pay their profits into a company in the Netherlands and in exchange for that, they have agreed they would not move the finishing process out of London."

"But, Holmes, their sales are made in this country, their manufacturing is carried out in this country. Surely they should be paying their taxes in this country?"

"This is what is known as a diversion of profits. The company pays a royalty to a company in the Netherlands which wipes out its British profits and accordingly it pays no tax in this country. The company in the Netherlands pays its profits to a company in a tax haven so no taxes are due in the Netherlands either. The profits therefore accrue in the tax haven. The British company then borrows against its balances in the tax haven to pay its dividends. It is sometimes called a Dutch sandwich because most of these arrangements work through the Netherlands as the Dutch allow payments of this kind into tax havens without a withholding tax. The London Softwear Company has clearly just agreed such a deal with the Chancellor in return for keeping its factory in Bloomsbury open."

"But Mr Lawler will be pleased by the result as the factory will continue to employ a large workforce in his constituency."

"We shall see. I will send a note around to him to come to Baker Street tomorrow. I shall ask him for twelve noon to make it easier for you to join us. I would not be without my Boswell for a case like this."

Mr Lawler was as punctual as ever. When Holmes explained the deal that London Softwear had been in the process of making with the Chancellor, a mixture of confusion and anger came across his face. "While I am delighted for my constituents that the jobs at the factory are likely to be saved, and would also congratulate you on your new appointment, Dr Watson, I am outraged that a major company should be able to blackmail the government on its tax bill in this way. Only a big company could do this. It is not as though …" – and I could see Mr Lawler trawling his mind for a wildly improbable example to illustrate his objection to London Softwear's practices – "… a small London coffee shop could claim that there is a special coffee-bean roasting technique for which it must pay royalties to a company overseas. Such a thing is preposterous!"

"I take it there is no other matter you wish to pursue on this case, Mr Lawler?" asked Holmes.

Lawler sat back in his seat and pondered.

"I wonder," he said at length, "how widespread such deals really are between major companies and the British government. I would be interested in raising a question about it in the Houses of Parliament. Would you be able to provide me with help on that score, Mr Holmes? And, as always, I would welcome your assistance in this, Dr Watson. The honest and overburdened British taxpayer needs protection from such predatory practices."

When Mr Lawler had gone, I turned to Holmes. "How are we going to investigate something like this?"

"We will have to make a visit to one of the large firms of business advisers in the City. Let us go and get some business cards made up. Inspired by Mr Lawler's apparently random idea of a coffee retailer exporting its profit to a tax haven, I shall call myself

Mr Lysander Starr of Topeka, whose name you will associate with the small matter of the Three Garridebs, and claim to represent a chain of American coffee shops."

"But Holmes! You said there never was such a man!"

"Indeed so, Watson, and there never was such a chain of coffee shops. As a matter of equally arbitrary choice, let us style you as Mr Buck who can be Mr Starr's British business partner."

Not many hours had passed before, fitted out with business cards advertising Holmes and me as Mr Starr and Mr Buck, we ventured into the City of London. In a shorter space of time than I could have imagined possible, we found ourselves in the magnificently appointed offices of the famous City advisers, Pitt & Waterman, which command a splendid view over St Paul's Cathedral from their site on Pater Noster Square.

After we had presented ourselves at the reception, Holmes and I sat in the foyer looking at the firm's literature, which extolled its charitable work as well as providing a listing of clients. Holmes slipped a couple of the documents into his pocket. Very soon we were ushered into a spacious meeting room and found ourselves speaking to the firm's managing partner, the fair, slim, elegantly dressed Mr Christopher Marler.

Holmes led the conversation.

We wanted, Holmes explained, once initial pleasantries had been exchanged, to set up a chain of coffee shops to serve the City of London. We would serve artisan quality coffee made using beans that had been subject to a special proprietary roasting process, the owner of which was based in the Netherlands. What did Mr Marler think was an appropriate level of royalty the UK business should pay to the Dutch owner for the rights to the process?

"How much is the margin that you envisage each shop making?" asked Mr Marler.

"In the United States, our shops' margin runs at about thirty-eight per cent," said Holmes.

"I understand that is a fairly standard margin in businesses run by our American cousins, but I assume your British outlets would be mere purveyors to the public of this proprietary process which is housed in the Netherlands?"

"Yes," said Holmes cautiously. "It is certainly possible to perceive their role in that way. Roasting coffee beans using our technique is a complex task, whereas making cups of coffee with the roasted beans is, by comparison, a simple one."

"In fact," expanded Marler, "is it not possible to say that without the proprietary process, the shops would probably not exist and that, accordingly, the business's unique selling point sits outside British jurisdiction?"

"Once again, Mr Marler," said Holmes after some thought, "it is certainly possible to see matters as you describe."

"It is very hard for the mere sellers of coffee to show a significant margin, Mr Starr. Competition in the sector is fierce and it is only by means of the proprietary process, the ownership of which sits in the Netherlands, that you are able to show a significant level of profit. The Dutch owner of the process is surely entitled to his share of the reward. I can see no reason why your coffee shops should pay a royalty of less than, shall we say, thirty-seven per cent of revenue to reflect this."

"And will there be no one to challenge that level of royalty?" I asked.

"If your company additionally gives us the mandate to act as your statutory auditors, Mr Buck, then we will hardly be in a position to say that the royalty deal was not transacted at arm's length."

"But surely," I responded to Mr Marler in some confusion, "your audits are conducted by clerks and their supervisors, who have wide-ranging commercial experience, while the audit team will include specialists in the business sector our company will operate in. With their depth of knowledge, they will be able to assess the level of the royalty's appropriateness for the complexity of the process and also to compare it to similar arrangements in other companies. This would enable them to query whether our royalty reflects an arm's-length transaction which would be a requirement if it is to be a taxable expense?"

"My dear Mr Buck," said Mr Marler, "the so-called front end of our audits are conducted by people with no business experience at all. They have normally barely completed their education. They are required to conduct the audit to a tight time-scale and the last thing they want to do is exercise any commercial judgement such as deciding whether a transaction between related parties is at a fair valuation. They would then require time-consuming clearance of it at a senior level and this would prevent them completing their work in line with their budget."

"So if your staff are, in fact, not seasoned businessmen, how can they perform an audit?"

"For a cash business like yours, Mr Rogers, our staff will check the cash, make sure that no large supplier invoices relating to the previous period have been received in the first three months of the following financial year and ..." – Mr Marler paused here to take a pinch of snuff, and I assumed he would continue to outline further audit steps, but instead he continued – "... that is all they will need to do to satisfy themselves that your accounts show a true and fair view. One of our partners will then sign off the accounts based upon the evidence that is presented to him."

"So does that not make your audit rather generic? Does that not mean that anyone would be capable of carrying out such a service?"

"On the contrary, Mr Rogers; our audit approach is a highly individual one. It was devised in the Netherlands and this firm is required to pay a hefty royalty there in order to be able to make use of it. Indeed, in order to pay the partners here any profit share at all, the firm has entered into substantial borrowings and has to provide heavy security to its lender in the form of overseas deposits."

"And will her Majesty's tax inspectors not be inquisitive about our activities and indeed about yours?"

"The firm of which I am proud to be a partner conducts a quarter of the audits of major companies in this country," said Mr Marler loftily. "Due to the recent government efficiency drive, the number of tax inspectors is at an all-time low and their pay has not been increased for the last five years. I should be most surprised if they had the resources to investigate you and even more surprised if they had the stomach. To do so would call into question the probity of the accounts of every company in the country and suggest that His Majesty's Inspectors' past scrutiny of them has been indigent in the extreme. Indeed, the thought that any tax inspector or anyone else with any association with tax collection might cross our own threshold for any purpose other than to apply for a position here is entertaining," Mr Marler paused to take another pinch of snuff, "but utterly preposterous."

Holmes rose and said to Mr Marler: "Your insights have been most illuminating. We will be sure to involve your firm in our next steps."

"Please feel free to do so," said Mr Marler with a bow as we took our leave. "You will find our charges are levelled at a rate at least as competitive as the rate of charges levelled by our competitors."

"What did you make of that?" I asked Holmes as we headed towards North London.

"For the first time in my life," replied he, looking a little downcast, "I find myself cursing the uniqueness of my intellect. I seem to be the only person in the land who really cannot claim that the intellectual property which drives my business is housed in the Netherlands. My intellectual property is self-evidently housed in my own skull, which is immutably located in London and which is where I conduct most of my cases."

I had been wondering if I should ask Holmes's advice on whether I could claim that my fledgling medical practice had intellectual property in the Netherlands and could accordingly pay royalties there to obviate the requirement of paying tax in Great Britain. Given his comment, I thought better of it. Instead I asked him why American businesses apparently still showed a genuine commercial margin in their accounts while for British companies such margins seemed to be a matter of altruistic choice.

"American companies," said Holmes, "are taxed on their worldwide income so there is no benefit for them in diverting their profits to different, more sympathetic jurisdictions. Doubtless they find other ways of rendering their tax liabilities nugatory."

I asked him what he was going to say to Mr Lawler.

"We shall have to inform Mr Lawler that the sort of practices the London Softwear Company are engaged in are standard in British commerce. Given the facility with which it is possible to make such an arrangement, the shareholders of London Softwear are even entitled to ask why the company did not avail itself of this set-up earlier. The directors of a company are under a fiduciary duty to minimise its tax liability and in fact Mr Velder and Mr Alleyne appear to have been somewhat dilatory in this matter if their business has been going for five years and they are only now considering such a step. This may be why Alleyne feels his position is under threat even if this scheme they are discussing with the Chancellor enables the company to avoid taxes."

I joined Holmes the next afternoon in Baker Street and Mr Lawler arrived at the appointed hour.

"Your endeavours have again been of great service to me, Mr Holmes," he said after Holmes had appraised him of the situation. "A stand must be taken against this. I shall go into battle armed with the sword of justice in my hand and the interests of the British taxpayer in my heart. Thrice armed is he who knows his cause is just. I am sure there will be great interest in making the public aware of what is happening."

"Might you not cause problems for your constituents if your efforts cause the setting aside of the arrangement London Softwear has arrived at with the Chancellor and the consequent closure of the factory? And might not any exposure of this arrangement render the position of your Chancellor difficult?"

"Politics, my dear Mr Holmes," said Lawler smoothly, "is the art of the possible. There is nothing more to say, but much still to do."

He picked up the dossier on the case which Holmes offered to him and, with a sweeping bow, he was gone.

The next day, *The Daily Telegraph* carried a front-page story about the arrangements certain companies had made to minimise their tax liabilities. Under the headline, "A Fraud on the Taxpayer", the newspaper ran an article of which the first paragraph read as follows:

> "Large corporations have the ability to agree with the government an amount that the latter will settle for rather than the amount that would be due if the tax were calculated on the true amount of revenue less a fair deduction of expenses. A basic British principle of justice is equality before the law. How can this be upheld when tax liabilities for large corporations are arrived at based on arbitrary agreements reached behind closed doors in smoke-filled rooms, whereas small companies pay the full rate? Such arrangements are an affront to natural justice."

The article went onto name a number of companies who had made such deals with the government although the London Softwear Company was not among those named. I had every idea where *The Telegraph* had its core information for the article from, but no idea how it had identified the companies which had benefited from the arrangements it was condemning. It was many months later when I was writing up this case from my notes that Holmes helpfully pointed out what excellent use Mr Lawler had made of the client list of Pitt and Waterman, which was in the dossier which Holmes had prepared and that Mr Lawler had taken with him.

A government spokesman issued a statement to say that no further special deals would be entered into and that all the present ones were subject to review.

For all the political upheavals, I still had my house to maintain and my wife to keep. Accordingly, I decided to keep my appointment at London Softwear that day, even though I realised it was possible that the directors would gather the work force in the central courtyard on the pretext of celebrating the company's success only to tell them that their employment was being terminated. I now saw the cordoning-off of the central courtyard and my appointment as Company Doctor entirely from the point of view that Holmes had articulated. Given the precautions the company seemed to be taking against the workers' possible reaction to their termination, I was filled with dread as to how they might respond and had the darkest visions of what revenge they might wreak on the person of anyone who seemed to them to be in a position of authority.

I walked through the arch into the central courtyard and, as I did so, I heard the leaden sound of carriage wheels behind me which, when I turned round to look, I saw came from heavy windowless coaches which were being drawn by massive Shire horses. The coaches drew up in the cordoned-off area of the courtyard. The fountain, I noted, had been encased in a protective structure of a robustness which to my eyes was utterly disproportionate for the winter covering of a water-feature.

With my misgivings further increased, I presented myself at the reception and asked for Mr Alleyne.

"He is due to come down at any moment. The workforce is being gathered in the courtyard for a major announcement," said the receptionist.

As I looked at the various corporate notices on the wall, I observed that none of them related to anything after 31 December 1907. I was about to look for an excuse to leave when I heard the sound of footsteps and I turned to see Mr Alleyne coming down the stairs.

"It is good to see you, Dr Watson," he said. "We are just gathering the workforce for the announcement and it will be of great benefit to have a doctor standing by as well as the additional outside support we have gathered to ensure that everything runs smoothly."

The workforce slowly gathered from the factory floor and I noticed that they had to make their way around the sealed carriages which ominously seemed to be parked in front of the entrances to the shop floor. My heart beat harder against my ribs as Mr Alleyne stood on a dais to address the crowd, with Mr Velder next to him. Was it a coincidence or was it part of the planning that the dais was right next to the archway leading to the street and therefore facilitated a swift egress?

"I have called you away from the shop floor," began Mr Alleyne, "to make a number of important announcements. We are committed to securing the best conditions for you, our work force, to whom the success of this business belongs. From today, this company will benefit from the services of Dr John Watson of Queen Square, who has agreed to become the Company Doctor and will ensure the highest possible healthcare standards are offered to you all."

I waved nervously to the crowd, who were kind enough to applaud politely as I identified myself. My heart continued pounding painfully against my ribs as I waited for the next part of the announcement.

"We have been in negotiations," continued Mr Alleyne, "with a number of different parties about the future of this site." Now a murmur of disquiet spread through the ranks of burly workers and I could feel my temples throbbing as my blood coursed through the engorged veins. "Among these parties," Mr Velder went on, "is the North London Development Board. They have been persuaded by our success to give us a generous grant to enable us to buy the machinery that is used to make the garments to which you have been so brilliantly applying the special London Softwear Company finish. This will expand our business here and you will soon be joined by another five hundred staff."

There was a lusty cheer from the workforce and my heartbeat suddenly returned to a normal pulse.

"And finally," concluded Mr Alleyne, "today marks precisely five years since the opening of this site. On behalf of the board I am happy to invite you to lay down your tools for this one afternoon and to join us in a celebration catered for by the St Giles Brewery, whose carriages you can see around us. We are indeed blessed that the weather is remarkably clement for the time of year, so that we can have this celebration outside. Drinks of all sorts will be served and I would beg you to go home after the festivities are over. It would be unfortunate indeed if Dr Watson's first task as Company Doctor were to be to have to cut out someone out of the compressor – indeed I am not even sure he has got a bone cutter with him in his medical bag." He paused as a nervous titter rippled through the workforce. "But in any case, it is a happy coincidence that Dr Watson is here on site in case any celebrations get a little bit out of hand."

Mr Alleyne concluded his speech shortly afterwards to a hearty ovation and the festive mood then got into full swing as the caterers appeared from the sealed carriages.

Mr Lawler suddenly appeared at my elbow and beamed conspiratorially at me. "I told you that politics was the art of the possible, Dr Watson!" he said. "It was I who arranged for the company to receive a grant from the North London Development Board for the purchase of new machinery. And because this will result in a significant increase in the number of people employed and greater prosperity of the workforce, the local council has also agreed to waive all property taxes on the company for the next twenty years, on condition that production continues here. You can see some of the machinery has arrived already," and he pointed to some large packing cases being unloaded from a carriage which had just driven into the courtyard. "This development is of benefit to us all."

I stayed at the London Softwear Company's premises until all but the last few workers had departed for home. As I left, I passed the packing cases and noted they were carrying despatch notes from Manchester.

I picked up an evening paper on the way home which carried the sensational news that the Chancellor of the Exchequer was standing down due to the publicity surrounding the special tax deals given to large companies. "When the person of the Chancellor rather than the success of the economy becomes the story," the Chancellor was quoted as saying in his letter of resignation, "then it is time for someone else to take over. I wish Mr Lawler every success in his new role as Chancellor of the Exchequer." A paragraph further down, speculating on future roles for the Chancellor, mooted the possibility of a consulting role for him with one of the financial advice companies and Pitt & Waterman was specifically mentioned. "A radical tax-reforming chancellor such as this one is well-placed to point advisers in the direction where maximum tax efficiency can be achieved."

Within a few weeks, I was reflecting that it was not just Mr Lawler who was among the financial beneficiaries of Holmes's latest case. After a quiet start for my practice, the regular additional income from the enlarged London Softwear Company operations, allied to the income I derived from those members of the workforce who subsequently became my patients, proved the bedrock of my business. Accordingly, I was soon able to reward my wife with the shopping expedition she craved to one of the great fashion emporia in Knightsbridge.

On our arrival, she observed immediately that the advertising line to call shoppers' attention to where London Softwear's products were laid out had changed. "It used to say 'Garments imported from Amsterdam, finished in London'," she commented thoughtfully. "Now it says, 'Finished according to a secret Dutch process'."

She paused to try a couple of outfits on. "And perhaps they don't look quite so good and they certainly don't feel so comfortable as they did when they were imported. And they are just as expensive as they ever were. Maybe to protect your purse, John, I shall have to try on some competitor products." And she moved into the next aisle to investigate.

A New Line of Attack

This story is in many ways the most multi-faceted of all the ones I have chosen to place before the public. It provides a startling insight into the workings and priorities of the British Government at the start of the 1930s and highlights a lost opportunity to use Holmes's great intellect on a task for which it would have been uniquely suited. It also showcases my friend's speed in acquiring a mastery of a field of activity which was completely alien to him. So great was this mastery that he was able to provide strikingly original and successful ideas to experts in that field, which were used to undermine the only living man whose expertise, albeit in a sphere outside detective work, my friend recognised as the equal of his own. Finally, I can adduce no other case which so well demonstrates the keenness of my friend's senses. But Holmes's capabilities were not always put to the best possible use by those who had the opportunity to do so and, as my reader will discover, nowhere is this truer than here.

The year 1930 had already been notable for two cases which I have related as "The Red Priest's Treasure Trove" and "The German Interpreter". While I had been delighted to resume my collaboration with Holmes after many years of only the most sporadic contact, I assumed by the second half of August of that year that there would be no more cases for a while and that the spurt of activity of that year had been an enjoyable aberration.

I was therefore surprised when in the early morning of Saturday, the sixteenth of August, I received a telegram from Holmes saying "MUST SEE YOU ON FINAL TEST". My reader will be aware of the grave matter I published under the title "The Final Problem", so I was both intrigued and concerned to find out what Holmes was referring to. Within a short space of time, I was looking into the keen eyes of my friend as he sat across the desk of my consulting room while he explained the commission with his customary clarity.

"It's like this, Watson," he said. "A Mr Jardine, who my archives have shown me to be both a businessman and an amateur sportsman of some distinction, has asked me for advice on a matter involving his sporting activities. This is not an arena where I have any knowledge at all and I was wondering if you would join me on this commission, in case there are technical matters on which I may require your assistance?"

"But Holmes!" I exclaimed, "Mr Jardine is one of the finest cricketers in the country. He has not been playing regularly this year, but two years ago he performed with great distinction on England's triumphant tour to Australia. I should be delighted to provide with you any assistance I can."

In less than an hour, Holmes and I were in the Committee Room at the Oval Cricket Ground, being introduced to the tall and spare Douglas Jardine.

"Today is the start of the final Test match of the summer against Australia," Jardine began. "Fitness and form permitting, I have been advised that I am likely to be asked to lead the England touring party to Australia in just over two years' time, even though I am not in the team at the moment. This is a signal honour for me as, to date, no Wykehamist has had the England captaincy bestowed on him."

"Pray continue."

"Australia have two players who have been outstanding all this summer. I was looking for some new insights from you, Mr Holmes, on a way to blunt their effectiveness in Australia in two years' time as, if we don't achieve this, we are not going to win. I appreciate from the work of your friend, Dr Watson here," and Jardine nodded towards me, "that what I am looking for is a slight departure from your normal area of expertise, but I feel that it is precisely the observations of the unencumbered mind that I am looking for."

"You live in a different world to me, Mr Jardine," said Holmes, "a sweeter and healthier one. My ramifications stretch out into many sections of society, but never, I am happy to say, into sport, which is the best and soundest thing in England and about which I know nothing."

Jardine's face fell at this comment. "So am I to understand," he asked in a downcast tone, "that you know nothing about the spectacle in front of us?"

Holmes looked out at the great green sward beneath us and the figures in white scattered across it. "Inasmuch as I have a sport at all," he said thoughtfully, "it is boxing which has on occasions been useful to me in my work. I make it my practice not to retain knowledge of topics that are not similarly useful. Accordingly, while I have some slight recollection of playing cricket at school, all I see before me are thirteen men dressed in white of whom two bear sticks and defend a target—"

"A wicket," I interjected.

"—against a ball propelled by one of the other eleven. Presumably they do that like a boxer defends his jaw, while seeking to strike the ball as a boxer strikes his opponent," continued Holmes. "Beyond that, however, I see a sporting spectacle, but have no more understanding of what I see than of what you would understand if you looked at a piece of undecrypted cipher."

"Well, Mr Holmes," said Mr Jardine, "I will try and enlighten you about the game. Let us go to our seats."

We sat in the second row of the top deck of the pavilion looking down on the play. The sun shone and the ground was full. Looking around me I could see several distinguished guests of Surrey County Cricket Club. The Prince of Wales, the club's patron, was in the row in front of us watching the play, and I noted, among the large party with him, both the Chancellor of the Exchequer, Philip Snowden, and the former Home Secretary, Sir John Simon.

"Cricket," began Jardine, "is played between two teams of eleven players. One side, in this case England, is batting and endeavours to score points or so-called runs either by running between the two targets or striking the ball to the boundary – the piece of rope you can see at the edge of the grass – after it has been propelled by the bowler."

I must admit here to letting my attention wander as Jardine continued his explanation of a game I knew well. I noted to my amusement that the Prince was also trying to explain the game of cricket to a group of American ladies in his party and seemed to be having many of the same difficulties with them as Jardine was having with Holmes.

"The other team," I heard Jardine continue after Holmes had asked a series of questions which betrayed only a lack of understanding of the game, "propels or delivers the ball in such a way as to make it difficult for the batting side to achieve this and with the objective of making the batsman commit an infraction such as letting his wicket be struck by the ball, or having the ball caught directly from the bat. When this happens, the batsman is replaced by one of his teammates. Once all the players of the first side have batted, the other team goes in and seeks to exceed the tally of runs made by the first team. The team that scores the most runs and dismisses the batsmen of its opponents wins the game."

"You make yourself very plain," said Holmes and watched for a few minutes, puffing contentedly on his pipe, before he made another remark.

"So presumably," he said finally as we watched a tall figure running in, "the difficulty posed by this ball propeller—"

"Bowler," I offered.

"—is the velocity with which he propels the ball?"

"Yes," said Jardine. "That is Tim Wall, who is the fastest bowler on the Australian team."

We watched a little longer and the small, wizened and becapped Grimmett came on to bowl from the other end.

"And presumably the difficulty posed by this bowler," said Holmes, after Grimmett had bowled his first two balls, "is that he sometimes makes the ball spin clockwise and sometimes widdershins so that when it lands, it sometimes moves into the batsman like the first delivery and sometimes moves away like the second?"

I saw Jardine start violently at this comment by my friend. "Mr Holmes!" he exclaimed. "How, in the name of all that's wonderful, do you know that? I know from my own experience of facing Grimmett that his ability to turn the ball both ways with little discernible change of action is the principal difficulty he causes, but a few minutes ago you were displaying no understanding of cricket at all."

"Are you telling me, Mr Jardine," replied Holmes, sounding somewhat taken aback, "that your eyesight is not of a level to enable you to see that the ball is sometimes rotating one way out of Grimmett's hand and sometimes in the opposite direction? Perhaps it is as well that, as your lack of a tan indicates, your main focus this summer has been on your business interests rather than on sport. We are no more than ninety yards away from Grimmett and the difference in the direction of rotation of the ball as it spins through the air is obvious." He turned to me, "Watson, I have done you a disservice. I have commented that you see but do not observe. I would question whether Mr Jardine even sees. Mr Jardine, is acuity of vision not generally an important requisite for players of this game?"

The Surrey amateur was clearly not used to being addressed in this cavalier fashion and I could see him chewing on the stem of his pipe after Holmes's last remark, but he again mastered himself to say: "Indeed, Mr Holmes, my eyesight appears not to be at your level. But if none of our players can see the direction in which the ball spins out of Grimmett's hand – even if you can – that will not give them very much help."

"But surely it is entirely predictable," said Holmes, as the Australian spin bowler ran in to bowl the next one, "that Grimmett will spin this one anti-clockwise." We paused as Oldfield, the wicketkeeper crouching behind the wicket, moved to his right to collect the ball as it turned and spun past the outside edge of the batsman's hesitant grope forward.

Jardine's face had gone from expressions of hope to scepticism and then to wonder within a few seconds. "Mr Holmes!" he exclaimed. "Can you see some change in Grimmett's run-up between his different kind of deliveries?"

Holmes held his counsel for several minutes as Grimmett and Wall continued bowling in tandem. Finally, he said:

"My dear Mr Jardine! It must be evident to you that the man squatting behind the wicket—"

"The Australian wicket-keeper, Oldfield," I chimed in.

"—has to know which way the ball is spinning so that he can gather it. If none of the England players can follow the rotation of the ball in the air, then nor can he. Is it possible that you have not spotted how Grimmett signals his intentions of which way he is going to spin the ball to Oldfield?"

We sat and watched for a while before Holmes explained his inference with an air of barely concealed impatience. “When Grimmett is going to rotate the ball anti-clockwise, he turns anti-clockwise before he runs in to bowl. And when he intends to rotate the ball clockwise, he turns clockwise before he runs into bowl. That is how Oldfield knows in which direction he needs to move to gather the ball.”

As the play progressed, we saw Grimmett turn anti-clockwise for eleven deliveries in a row. But on the twelfth he turned clockwise. The clockwise delivery had Oldfield move sharply but smoothly to his left to take the ball down the leg side.

“Mr Holmes!” exclaimed Jardine. “Your deductions surpass even the expectations created by the writings of your chronicler, Dr Watson here. Grimmett is one of the people on whom I wanted to seek your advice as he has been by far the most dangerous of the Australian bowlers this summer. Armed with this knowledge, however, I think we may be able to counter him. I shall talk to the England captain as soon as the opportunity presents itself.”

Shortly before the tea break, England’s fifth wicket fell with only one hundred and ninety-seven on the board as Grimmett bowled Leyland for three to gain his second wicket of the innings and his twenty-sixth of the series. Jardine disappeared at tea time but he returned in time for the restart.

“Well, you have fixed one problem, Mr Holmes,” said Jardine with an air of grim determination as shortly before the close Wyatt clubbed another delivery from the Australian spinner dismissively to the boundary. “That’s knocked the stuffing right out of Grimmett.” A few minutes passed before he spoke again. “But the second member of the duumvirate I need you to stop is the man down there.”

He pointed to a slim blond figure fielding on the boundary close to the pavilion. As we watched, Donald Bradman sprinted round to intercept another booming drive from Wyatt off Grimmett just short of the rope and turned an apparently obvious four into just a single.

“Tomorrow is a rest day,” continued Jardine, “but on Monday it is likely that Bradman will bat and I would be grateful for your insights on him. We have found this man almost impossible to dislodge all summer and I hope your comments on him are as insightful as your ones on Grimmett.”

No more wickets fell in the evening session and England closed at three hundred and sixteen. We agreed to meet on the Monday when it was likely that Bradman would bat to see what further wisdom Holmes could impart.

I had expected Holmes to come back to my house in Queen Square after we left the ground, but he expressed a preference for his cottage on the South Downs and we parted at Vauxhall Station.

I was preparing to go back to the ground on Monday morning when a telegram arrived from Holmes. "BUSY WITH ARCHIVES. WILL COME TOMORROW."

I had no idea why archives might be such an impediment to Holmes coming to the second day, but I let Jardine know by telegram that we could not join him at the Oval until the Tuesday. In our absence, England closed on four hundred and five with Grimmett taking two tail-end wickets and, after a fine opening stand, Australia finished the second day on two hundred and fifteen for two with Bradman twenty-seven not out.

On the Tuesday morning, Holmes and I met at the Oval. Jardine sent a message saying he had a business appointment, but promising to join us after lunch. Through his father, who was on the club committee, we again had seats at the top of the pavilion. I sat in wonder as Holmes demonstrated that his time in his archives had not been spent without purpose, although the beginning of the exposition of his findings sounded unpromising in the extreme:

"You will remember Isonomy who was in the direct bloodline that produced Silver Blaze," Holmes began. "Isonomy only ran fourteen times, but won ten of the races he ran – an extraordinary win rate well beyond almost any horse. His owner, Fredrick Gretton, withheld him from major races so that when the stallion ran in the Cambridgeshire Handicap at Newmarket, the odds against him were 40–1 and his win thereby delivered Gretton a massive financial coup. This sort of thing is possible in a sport where there are owners who can control when their horses run and so a newcomer can blaze onto the scene and defy the normal law of statistical performance."

"And how does this bear on Don Bradman?" I asked, confused as to how the performance of a horse could be of relevance to the performance of a cricketer like Bradman.

"Bradman's performances," Holmes explained, "also defy the normal laws of statistics. But cricket, by contrast with horse-racing, is a game where there is little scope for performances outside the normal laws of statistics once a meaningful sample is used. It is widely played, there is no motivation to hide a player's performance, no one to hide it for him, and its scoring methodology, more than that of any other sport, delivers a huge fund of statistics by which you can reasonably compare the achievements of different players. Accordingly, I would expect its performers to conform to a normal range of performance and scatter."

He paused to reach into a folder and drew out a piece of foolscap which was covered with figures in his small, neat writing.

"Instead," he continued, "I find that Bradman's statistics put him off the statistical scale. In the last Australian domestic season, the average score by all batsmen who played was twenty-seven with a standard deviation of ten. You would therefore expect the most extreme performances to fall within three standard deviations of this." Holmes picked up his score-card and drew a small chart with a Gaussian curve of deviation from the mean to illustrate his point. "McCabe, the second-best batsman in Australia, is almost exactly three deviations from the mean. He averaged fifty-six – just under three standard deviations from the mean of all Australian batsmen last year." Holmes put a little cross on the extreme right-hand edge of the bell curve to illustrate his point. "Bradman, by contrast, averaged one hundred and thirteen, which places him eight and a half deviations from the mean. So, if I take twenty-seven and ten as being representative mean and standard deviation for cricket at large, his average of ninety-three in his Test matches to date is over six and a half standard deviations from the mean." Holmes marked another cross on his score-card, this time well outside the bell-shape of his Gaussian curve.

I looked out at the slight Bradman as he stood at the crease. He had already advanced his score to over a century by lunchtime. I was surprised to note that Holmes was equally engrossed.

"I remain the world's only consulting detective," he commented, seemingly unable to take his eyes off the spectacle below us, "and even after fifty years I am still a nonpareil in my field. Bradman would appear to be my equivalent at batting, like Shakespeare on the stage, or Bach in the concert-hall."

Rain set in at lunch and there was little play for the rest of the day. Jardine sent us a message that he would join us the next day. On the Wednesday the three of us sat in our familiar seats in the pavilion and watched as Bradman advanced from his overnight score of one hundred and thirty. Many of the same people, including the party of important personages who had been present on Saturday, had returned on the Wednesday, presumably in the hope of seeing Bradman play a long innings. When he was on one hundred and seventy, he was struck over the heart by Larwood who was bowling at full pace and the Australian collapsed briefly to his knees.

Flushed with excitement, Jardine stood up from his seat and exulted. “But the blighter’s yellow! He’s yellow through and through!”

I could see a look of shock spread across the faces of the people around us at Jardine’s vulgar outburst, but Bradman himself rapidly recovered his poise from the blow he had been struck. He batted serenely on before falling for two hundred and thirty-two, which left his average for his seven innings in the series at one hundred and thirty-nine, or – as Holmes put it much to Jardine’s puzzlement – just over eleven standard deviations from the mean.

Australia closed two hundred and ninety ahead. In the interval between innings, the discussions between Holmes and Jardine, to which I was an observer, focused on how Bradman might be stopped.

"You have now seen Bradman play an innings, Mr Holmes. Have your sharp eyes spotted something that has to date escaped the attention of England's bowlers and their captain?"

Holmes hauled out his figure-covered sheet of foolscap. He first of all repeated for Jardine's benefit what he had told me about how extreme Bradman's performances were from a statistical point of view. I suspect that had Holmes not made his brilliant observations about Grimmett on the previous Saturday, Jardine would have made his excuses and left, but I could see he was hanging onto my friend's every word. Holmes continued:

"Bradman has yet to play enough at an international level for it to be statistically significant, even though it is worth pointing out that he now averages nearly one hundred and three after the first innings of his ninth Test, which is quite unprecedented. Instead of watching here, I have spent two days in my archives checking facts from newspapers and sending regular telegrams to Mr Wilder who, as Dr Watson will remember, fled to Australia under something of a cloud, and who accordingly was most anxious to help me in any way he could. For my statistical population, I looked at Bradman's innings in Australia, of which he has played fifty. These are the most relevant games as it is in Australia that you will be playing in three winters' time. In these fifty innings, his average is over ninety, which is also unparalleled."

"I had expected suggestions from you, Mr Holmes," said Jardine, looking at Holmes with the awed reverence I had only previously seen on the face of Stanley Hopkins, "on what bowlers to use and what fields to set. But there are very few easy one-per-cent gains left to make in cricket these days and statistical analysis is something we have not looked at before. Accordingly, I am most eager to hear your results."

"In his fifty innings, Bradman is a notably good completer of innings and a notably poor starter. In his top quartile of innings, he averages two hundred and ninety-eight and in the bottom quartile, he averages less than four. Nearly a third of his innings end before he has exceeded twenty."

Jardine drew contemplatively on his pipe before he asked "And how does that compare to other major batsmen?"

"I have compared Bradman against the Test match performances to date of Sutcliffe and Hobbs. For Sutcliffe, his bottom quartile of innings averages thirteen and his top quartile one hundred and thirty-eight. Four fifths of his innings exceed twenty. For Hobbs, the equivalent figures are nine and one hundred and thirty while over seven tenths of his innings exceed twenty. This means that compared to Hobbs and Sutcliffe, you have a good chance of getting Bradman early, but if he gets through the early skirmishes, his concentration is almost unshakeable."

"So what should my strategy be against him?"

"If his concentration is weaker at the beginning of his innings, it is perhaps best to try and disrupt it. Some sort of distraction tactic may be called for."

I could see Jardine looking a little sceptical at Holmes's suggestions, but the statistical confirmation of Bradman's superiority over all other batsmen gave the Surrey amateur little choice but to listen.

"And what sort of bowlers get him out cheaply?" he asked at length.

"In his bottom quartile of innings, there was one run out but, other than that, it is noticeable that he is as susceptible to fast bowling as he is to spin bowling in the initial phases of his innings. Among spin bowlers he is as vulnerable to wrist spinners as to finger spinners, irrespective of the direction in which they turn the ball – Grimmett, Blackie and White have all had successes against him. It is thus his concentration early in his innings that is suspect, not his technique against any bowling."

"But I have a theory that he is weak against fast bowling."

"I was going to raise this with you myself. I have not seen enough propellers of the ball—"

"Bowlers," I interrupted.

"—to carry out statistical checks of the type that I was able to perform on Bradman to assess the extent to which Larwood outpaces other bowlers. On my viewing in this game, however, he is notably faster than Australia's Wall, Fairfax and McCabe, and none of the English bowlers are close to being a match for him in terms of speed either. It was a remarkable feat for Larwood to have struck Bradman with the ball when the Australian had already reached one hundred and seventy, for my research has suggested that Bradman is virtually impossible to discommode when he has accumulated a score of that size. The precise matter I wanted to raise with you concerns the curious incident of the game between Nottinghamshire and the Australians at the beginning of July."

Holmes pulled a newspaper cutting out of his pocket and Jardine seized it eagerly to see what Holmes was referring to. After a few seconds of study of the cutting, he looked up at Holmes in puzzlement.

"But Bradman did not play for the Australians against Nottinghamshire in July. His name is not listed on this score-card."

"That was the curious incident," said Holmes mildly. "I would posit that Bradman was absent because in Larwood, Voce and Barratt, Nottinghamshire had the fastest attack in the country and that Bradman prevailed upon his captain not to choose him. As it was, Larwood and Voce got seven wickets between them in the Australians' first innings. The Australians had to bat out for a draw in the second and were helped by Nottinghamshire barely bowling Larwood."

"So it is not just Bradman who is yellow!" exclaimed Jardine so loudly as to attract the interest of our fellow spectators once again – but rather than calling Bradman by name, he used a term to describe him which I could not possibly repeat even in a story not intended for general publication until some point in the distant future. "The whole lot of them are cowards! … Well," he continued, "I'll make sure we make the most of that. We'll take a battery of fast bowlers out to Australia and pepper them with bowling on the line of the body. If their batsmen get hit, we'll call it regrettable collateral damage."

"I noted in my scrutiny of the archives," continued Holmes, after a brief pause following Jardine's outburst, "that Voce has not yet represented England."

"That will be remedied," replied Jardine, once he had calmed down. "There is a tour of the West Indies this winter and I will make representations to ensure that Voce goes on it. He needs to get experience of international cricket in hot conditions and this is his chance. As well as Larwood and Voce, we'll take Bowes and Allen to Australia. We saw Bradman struck on the body today. He and his teammates can look forward to plenty more of that. And that won't be the end of it. When we bowl the ball down the leg side, we'll pack the field, so that the blighters have no choice other than to hit the ball to the fieldsman or be hit. I greatly appreciate your suggestions, Mr Holmes. If anything else occurs to you, please be sure to let me know."

Holmes then asked in his mildest voice the question that was coursing through my head. "Do you not think your new line of attack on Bradman might generate some controversy in cricketing circles? I understand it is normal in cricket to attack the wicket rather than the body?"

"Laws were made for man, not man for laws," said Jardine in a voice which invited no argument. "What is anticipated does not breach the laws of our great game and, if we want to beat a team with a player who breaks the normal laws of statistical achievement, we have little choice."

England reduced the deficit by twenty-four before the end of the day's play.

Holmes and I walked to the station. On the way I raised the issue with him of the tactics that Jardine was going to pursue.

"Are they consistent with sportsmanship and good relations with the Australians?" I asked.

Holmes paused before replying:

"As Mr Jardine said, such tactics are within the laws of the game as at present constituted. I am, however, inclined to fear, especially if Mr Jardine is incautious enough to express some of the views in Australia that he has expressed to us and, in particular, if he chooses to employ some of the turns of phrase we have heard him use this afternoon, that, while he may win us the series, he may also lose us a dominion."

We parted at Vauxhall and Holmes showed no interest in returning the following day as Australia recovered the Ashes by bowling England out for two hundred and fifty-one. It was noticeable that Grimmett was largely ineffective when, on a pitch which had already been played on for four days, he might reasonably have expected some help. Hornibrook, by contrast, having taken a mere six wickets in the previous four games in the series, took seven here with his left-arm slow bowling.

I followed the cricketing scene over the next two and a half years running up to England's tour to Australia with the keenest interest and many events foreshadowed in what I have described so far duly came to pass. Voce had a successful tour of the Caribbean in 1930/31 while Jardine was appointed England captain in 1931. I also noted that for all Bradman's popular reputation, the Australian players were more inclined to attribute their success in 1930 to Grimmett than to Bradman. The Australian vice-captain, Richardson, was quoted as saying "We could have beaten anyone without Bradman. Without Grimmett we couldn't have beaten the blind school."

The English touring party for the 1932/33 tour of Australia, when it was announced, contained four out-and-out fast bowlers – Larwood, Voce, Bowes and Allen – as well as the brisk pace of

Wyatt. This provoked considerable surprise among cricket followers not armed with the conclusions Jardine had drawn following his encounter with Sherlock Holmes.

There was a long series of warm-up games between the tourists and various representative sides before the first Test match. Bradman had only indifferent success in the three of these games in which he played and in the third of them, he batted down the order. The newspaper reports I read described him as being ill, but the popular press gleefully pointed out that he had been able to play golf on the rest day. A stress-related complaint then caused him to miss the first Test match, which England won quite easily. I half-expected Bradman to stand down for the rest of the series, but he then returned for the second Test at Melbourne. I was fascinated to read the account of the first day's play in the *Daily Chronicle*, of which the following is an extract:

> O'Brien was run out when the Australian tally had reached sixty-seven. There was a roar from the crowd as Bradman came down the steps of the pavilion and made his way to the wicket. As he marked his guard, the roar continued. Bowes stood at his mark and made to start his run-up but the prolonged ovation made him pull out of it. Jardine gestured to the crowd, perhaps bidding them to be

still, but this only made the hubbub louder. Only after another whole minute had passed was Bowes finally able to move in. The Yorkshire paceman dropped the ball short and Bradman, perhaps distracted by the delay, went to hook. The ball cannoned off the bottom edge of the bat and onto the leg stump and Bradman was on his way, first ball. Jardine performed what looked like a somewhat undignified war dance at mid-on at his departure.

Although England eventually lost this game with Bradman scoring a not-out century in the second innings to maintain his Test-match batting average at over a hundred, I was not surprised at the efficacy of the tactics my friend had promulgated to Jardine.

The two teams next met at Adelaide. The tactic of fast bowling to a battery of leg-side fieldsmen had the consequences which were an inevitable risk of their implementation. One Australian player was hit over the heart and another had his skull broken. It was also noticeable how ineffective Grimmett had been throughout the series to date, and although the fourth Test post-dates the main events of this story, he was not selected for either of the last two Tests of the rubber. England won the Adelaide match by over three hundred runs to take the lead in the series and

Bradman scored sixty-six and eight to leave his average over the two Tests to date at fifty-nine.

I confess that my interest in the cricket reports on England's cricketing success in Australia rather overshadowed my interest in world events. I was consequently baffled when on the nineteenth of January 1933, I received a message in a sealed and highly embossed envelope, delivered by a dispatch rider, which demanded that I to report to the Foreign Office as soon as possible. I could only assume that such a summons must be the result of my connection with Sherlock Holmes, but I had no idea what new adventure I might be embarking on. When I arrived at the Foreign Office, I was asked into an ante room where Holmes was waiting.

"The Foreign Office asked me to come in on a matter of the utmost delicacy and I am reluctant to undertake something which might be of historical moment without my chronicler."

"And what is the matter on which they wish to consult you?"

"I have not yet been informed, but we are due to see the Foreign Secretary in a few minutes and doubtless all will be made clear."

Shortly afterwards, we were shown into a long conference room full of polished wood, silver and crystal. The suave figure of the Foreign Secretary, Sir John Simon, sat at the end of the table with two red boxes open in front of him. He closed them both as he rose to greet us.

We went through the process of making introductions. Sir John, I was aware, had a reputation for social gaucheness, but I was still surprised by a look of puzzlement which came come across his face as we sat down, and for several seconds he stared at us across the table. Finally, he reached into the red box nearest him, pulled out some papers and started to set out the issue on which he required our help.

"The matter I am going to set before you now, is of supreme importance," he eventually began. "You will recall how last year, the German President, Paul von Hindenburg, dissolved the German Parliament and called elections. There were two elections during the year – in July and September – in both of which the National Socialist German Workers' Party or NSDAP, led by Herr Adolf Hitler, received a significant plurality although their share of the vote fell from thirty-seven per cent to thirty-three per cent between the two elections. As they are still the largest party, there remains a significant danger of the National Socialist Party forming the major party in a German government."

"And what would be the likely outcome of a National Socialist administration?"

"The National Socialist party is revanchist in the extreme. They take seriously the legend of the stab in the back against the

German army on their western front in November 1918. They would almost certainly look to overturn the terms of the Versailles Treaty and to reverse the territorial changes that resulted from it, whether by use of direct force or by negotiations backed up by threats of military intervention in the newly established countries that border them. The consequences of such politics are unpredictable, but they are unlikely to be attractive."

"And has Hindenburg no other parliamentary options for forming a government?"

"The Chancellor, Schleicher, has used presidential decrees from Hindenburg to get legislation through the German Parliament and there have been numerous attempts at building an anti-Hitler coalition between what we would regard as more mainstream parties, but these have all been unavailing. There seem to be two constitutional options open to Hindenburg as the present impasse is not sustainable in a country whose economy is imploding. He can call for a third set of elections under which the National Socialists may well recover the votes they lost in November as people vent their anger at the exclusion from government of the largest party. They may even get a share of the vote above what they got in July. This would make the National Socialists' bargaining power even greater. Or he can permit a coalition with the present constellation of parties in the Parliament. This would either exclude Hitler's party from government, which would be a strange fate for the largest party in Parliament, or he could ask Hitler to form a government and seek to muzzle his powers by obtaining undertakings from him as to what he will do and not do. Hitler, of course, may or may not abide by any deal to which he agreed."

"But Germany was disarmed at the end of the Great War. Severe limitations have been put on its military capacity in any of the army, navy or air force and it is barred from having any troops on the west bank of the Rhine. We have within recent memory seen French and Belgian troops occupy parts of Germany. Is there no scope for military intervention from the West to impose a government of a more reasonable hue?"

"The French refuse to take the threat of Hitler seriously," said Simon in a sombre tone. "And this morning, I spoke to Viscount Hailsham, the Secretary of State for War. This country's military planning assumes no major hostilities for the next ten years and we are not in a position to send troops for what would be a major operation. Furthermore, our research into British public opinion indicates that there is no stomach for such an undertaking. The British public merely wishes to see potential German aggression contained. It does not wish to see the British army deployed to impose a government. There is no understanding in this country that failure to impose a moderate government may in fact lead to renewed German aggression at a later date."

"Could Hindenburg not use the remnants of the army to declare martial law and seize power himself?"

"There are a number of complicating factors preventing that. In the first case, Hindenburg is now well over eighty years old and his mental state is, at best, fragile. It may well be that he would be unwilling to do something of that nature against his own countrymen, or that he would be unable to survive the stress of doing so. Secondly, the National Socialist party has its own militia and its men are armed with all manner of irregularly obtained weapons. The German army is small, ill-equipped and demoralised. It is by no means clear that its members would prevail in a military action against the National Socialists, let alone that regular troops would show much heart for such a battle."

"So what is it you wish me to do?" asked Holmes at last.

"The Foreign Office," and Sir John paused to stare at us in apparent puzzlement for a second time, "was highly impressed by the speed and skill you showed in identifying the killer of Horst Wessel in Berlin three years ago. (Editor's note: covered in "The German Interpreter"). We have the gravest concerns about the consequences of what a government in Germany dominated by the National Socialists might mean. As a German speaker, you are an ideal candidate to travel to Germany and to investigate Hitler. We need to find out some tawdry personal scandal which could be used to undermine him, should word of it get out."

"What sort of thing did you have in mind?" asked Holmes.

"Let us take Oswald Mosley as a comparison," said Simon. "He has flitted from one political party to another and has risen to the top of each. He is a brilliant orator, and has a keen and cunning mind. These qualities make him one of the most dangerous men in the country. His present leadership of the British Union of Fascists is regarded as a serious threat to this country's safety. Our security services were sufficiently alarmed by him that they conducted a thorough investigation into his finances, as he has no obvious means of support. They found that much of his money comes from a most unlikely source."

"And that is?"

"He is the proprietor of a shop selling hosiery and designs many of its bestselling lines himself."

I glanced across at Holmes after this stunning revelation and could see surprise written over even his normally imperturbable countenance.

"Should the danger Mosley poses become too great," continued Sir John calmly but with an unmistakable hint of menace, "we are in a position to leak word of this to his followers who, we believe, would then seek to replace him as their leader. He is not aware of our knowledge of this, but we regard it as a key weapon against him, should the need arise."

"So," said Holmes, "may I summarise your brief? You wish me to travel to Germany and to uncover some hitherto unknown discreditable item of information about Hitler. Are the secret services not better equipped than I to deliver on this line of attack?"

"We need someone, Mr Holmes," and Sir John's eyes continued to look narrowly at Holmes, "on whom we can rely and who has a command of the language. We are not confident that there is anyone else who fits the bill."

"I am aware," said Holmes at length, "of rumours about Hitler's sexuality and of his ancestry. And a woman who was a relative of his was found dead in his Munich flat just over a year ago. I will be surprised indeed if there is nothing I can uncover about him which would make him unacceptable to his supporters or to the German population at large. Sir John, I relish this commission and would be happy to undertake an investigation of the type that you propose."

Our interview took not many more minutes before it was agreed that Holmes and I should travel together to Germany as soon as possible to see what could be found out. As we headed downstairs to the entrance of the Foreign Office I could see excitement etched on Holmes's face:

"I regard this as a chance to do some good for our country and for Germany!" he exclaimed. "Another conflagration is not in the interests of either of our nations and finding a way to undermine the bellicose Hitler is a good way to prevent it. I play the game for its own sake, but I cannot remember being so eager to fulfil a commission since I was asked to act as a double agent before the Great War."

We had just got to the top of the stairs leading down to the street of the Foreign Office when we were accosted by a uniformed messenger who had dashed after us:

"Sir John needs to speak to you again urgently," he panted between breaths.

We returned to the door of the conference room where we had just left Sir John. We were ushered in and without any formality or explanation Sir John asked: "Were you sitting in the second row of the top tier of the pavilion at the last Test match at the Oval in 1930?"

When Holmes said that he had been, Sir John said in no friendly tone "I was puzzling throughout our meeting to recall where I had seen you before. I summoned you to resolve a problem for me and I now realise you are the cause of another. As well as being Secretary of State for War, Lord Hailsham is the current President of the MCC. He was here this morning with a telegram he had received from the Australian Cricket Board."

Sir John reached into his second red box, picked out the telegram and read out to us: "'Bodyline bowling has assumed such proportions as to menace the best interests of the game, making protection of the body by the batsman the main consideration. This is causing intensely bitter feeling between the players, as well as injury. In our opinion it is unsportsmanlike. Unless stopped at once, it is likely to upset the friendly relations existing between Australia and England.'"

The Foreign Secretary put down the telegram and fixed us with a stare. "I overheard Jardine and someone I did not recognise discussing potential tactics for Australia," he finally said. "I now realise that the person who planted the seed in Jardine's head of aiming at the batsman's person rather than at the wicket and who has created an incident which threatens to split the Empire is you."

I could see Holmes was unsure how to respond to Sir John's remarks. Finally, my friend asked "So do you wish me to find a way to soothe Australian feelings rather than to travel to Germany to find out something discreditable about Hitler?"

"Thank you, Mr Holmes, I do not wish you to undertake any work for the Foreign Office at all. As I indicated to you, Foreign Office work requires people whose judgement may be relied upon and your intrigue with Jardine has shown that your judgement is not to be relied upon. I wish you a good day." Sir John touched a bell to summon a member of Foreign Office staff, who then escorted us from the building.

And so it was that a major opportunity to prevent Hitler's seizure of power was missed. He was sworn in as Chancellor on the thirtieth of January 1933. Meanwhile England went on to win the series against Australia by four matches to one at the expense of significant odium in Australia. Bradman's average for the series was fifty-six, or as Holmes might have put it had he shown any renewed interest in cricket, exactly three standard deviations from the mean. This is normally the outermost limit of what a human can achieve over any statistically meaningful period of time, but definitely a level of performance of normal mortals rather than that of a man operating beyond the bounds of normal statistical performance.

Before Holmes, no one else had been able to stop Bradman. I would like tentatively to suggest that if anyone could have stopped Hitler, who seemed to have a sixth sense for danger and dodged numerous attempts to assassinate him, it might have been my friend. As it was, Hitler had been voted dictatorial powers by the German electorate by the end of the following year with all the consequences that followed and the chance to use Holmes's preternatural abilities to stop him was gone.

At the same time, Anglo-Australian relations had recovered sufficiently that Australia returned to England's shores in 1934. Jardine had stood down as captain while Larwood and Voce were not selected.

Events in the series followed a similar pattern to 1930 with Australia winning a deciding Test at the Oval after Bradman had made another huge score. I have always wondered whether, in a bid to improve Anglo-Australian relations at a difficult time, Sir John

Simon, having recalled our discussions with Jardine, tipped the Australians off that England had spotted how Grimmett signalled his intentions to Oldfield of the direction in which he planned to spin the ball. In any event, the Australian spinner's fortunes were restored in 1934 and he took twenty-five wickets in the series, including seven in England's second innings at the Oval.

The Trial of Joseph Carr

"'Someone must have been slandering Joseph Carr,'" read our visitor, Miss Brusher, from a bulky document she had hauled out of her bag, "'as one morning, although he had not done anything wrong, he was arrested. The cook of his landlady, Mrs Gruber, who normally brought him his breakfast at eight a.m., did not appear. This had never happened before.'"

Miss Brusher had said she had come to consult about her fellow lodger's writings, which she found disturbing. She paused after her extraordinary opening, but was about to continue when Holmes broke in abruptly.

"Miss Brusher, have you really come here just to express concern about these writings of your neighbour? I can see no reason whatever why I, for whom time is of some value, should investigate something like this. Why, if you ask my fellow lodger, Dr Watson here, he will confirm that when I talk to him at all, it is mainly to point out his literary shortcomings. But that does not mean I propose to become a literary critic, and I see no point in adding your fellow lodger to the list of people whose writings I find wanting in true intellectual rigour."

"But, Mr Holmes," she countered. "If you will allow me to read you more of Mr Carr's writings, I can assure you that you will find them intriguing and grotesque."

My friend started at the word “grotesque”. “Watson!” he exclaimed. “That word again – for me it always carries an underlying suggestion of the tragic or terrible.”

Miss Brusher’s choice of words had made Holmes prepared to give her a longer audience. He laid down the Bunsen burner he had taken into his hand, reached for his pipe and sat back in his armchair with his eyes half-closed. “Pray tell me a little about yourself before you resume reading,” he requested.

“My name is Violet Brusher. I am a professional typist and live in lodgings at Prague Square. One of my fellow lodgers, Mr Joseph Carr, works in banking. Over the last few weeks he has taken to reading me what he claims is a book he is writing about his life. He has indeed become quite invasive in his attempts to read this work to me and has gone so far as to foist typescript onto me. While I am a woman who can look after herself, I find his writings so outlandish that I felt I should raise their content with someone in authority, but I am uncertain with whom. I then thought of you.”

She started reading again. The document she read from described the arrest and investigation of Joseph Carr. It was clear that Carr had been released although was still the subject of a process. Yet the narrative never stated any offence that he had committed or been accused of. It introduced characters such as Miss Brusher herself, other neighbours of Carr and figures associated with the arresting authority. Miss Brusher was reading a passage in which one of these was quoted as saying “The authorities, as far as I am aware – and I admit I am only a very minor cog in their machine – do not seek guilt in the population; rather they are attracted by guilt in the population and they have to send out us security staff,” when Holmes stopped her again.

“Miss Brusher, are you saying that some authority arrested your neighbour and that he has told you about this but that he has not told you on what charge, or by whom?”

“Mr Carr has told me nothing, sir, about why he was arrested or the authorities that arrested him beyond what is in this text.”

“This is very singular. We live in a country governed by a legal system and yet a man is arrested without charge by authorities whom he knows nothing about and yet still remains at liberty. It is almost as if these authorities are toying with him.”

The observation hung in the air as Miss Brusher continued. She read a passage where Carr had written “Once a week Carr visited a girl called Elsa, who worked as a waitress till the small hours and during the day only received guests in bed,” when Holmes called a peremptory halt.

“Miss Brusher, the text you are reading is very striking, but it is also extremely lengthy. Could you explain what you want me to do?”

Our client looked up. “Mr Holmes,” she said. “Mr Carr is in considerable personal distress. He badgers me both at home and at work with attempts to make contact with me. When I can no longer avoid him, he reads to me from this large and growing typescript. He is aging before my eyes and I feel the authorities he describes in this text are making his life impossible. This is rebounding onto me to such an extent that I have been constrained to take steps to avoid him altogether and accordingly I have asked a friend to share my room in the hope that Mr Carr will leave me alone when he sees I have company. At the same time, he writes about authorities I do not recognise but which seem to have a power over him such as that a state might have. I feel this matter should be raised with someone in authority, but I do not know with whom.”

“Miss Brusher, you place me in a very difficult position. On the one hand, you have no evidence that any real crime is taking place, or even that any of the events you talk about occur anywhere except in the imagination of Mr Carr. On the other hand, your fellow lodger’s writings suggest some gigantic conspiracy, though one of which I know nothing beyond what you have read out. You say that Mr Carr is oppressed by an authority which you have never heard of and yet suggest that this case may be something for the authorities. I suggest, as the entirety of your concerns rests with this tome-like typescript, you leave it with me and I will go through it thoroughly. I will revert to you when I have formed a plan of action, should one be required.”

"What did you make of her, Watson?" Holmes asked thoughtfully after our visitor had left.

I ventured "Pleasant, respectable, pretty, smartly turned out and deeply disturbed by her fellow lodger ..." before a snort from Holmes brought me to a halt.

"Really, Watson, how often do I have to remind you to look at detail and not merely state vague and, if I may make so bold, rather subjective impressions? The lady is obviously disturbed by the attentions of Carr – that is precisely what she said herself – but you are failing to look at the minutiae that demonstrate it and which illuminate other things about her and her surroundings. The streak of powder by her left ear, just where the light caught her, shows both her interest in theatre and her distraction in that she failed to remove it. The speck of brick dust on her blouse, just above the waist, shows it has been hung out of the window to dry and thus that there are no clothes-drying facilities at her lodgings. When you see an otherwise orderly person failing to remedy such flaws in their appearance, you can be sure that their attention is focused on something outside their normal sphere of activity."

"And what do you make of her problem?"

"My first idea was that it was some vulgar, romantic intrigue, as Carr always seems to accost Miss Brusher when she is on her own. The content of the typescript rules that out, however. No man would seek to make love to a lady by reading a document suggesting he was subject to a persecution by an unknown authority, let alone one detailing weekly visits to a lady who only receives visitors in bed during the day – at which point, you will note, I called Miss Brusher to a halt. I will have to dedicate further attention to the text that Miss Brusher has brought."

And, rather to my surprise, Holmes abandoned his chemical research and for the rest of the day said not a word to me as he sat hunched in his chair turning over the pages, puffing at his hookah, which was his closest companion in his moments of deepest introspection. He seemed focused not only on the words but also on the paper and sometimes took out a magnifying glass to look at it more closely. At one point he even put one page under his microscope and stared intently and at considerable length down the tube as greyish-blue tobacco smoke blew out ever more fiercely into our sitting room.

It was only when I was about to go to bed that he spoke any further words and even then they seemed to be addressed to himself.

"A perfectly unique document. As to where it leads us, I am still no clearer than when Miss Brusher arrived this morning. The core of this case is all contained in this text and, even after concentrating my attention on it all day, I remain undecided on whether this is a work of invention, a statement of events, or a conflation of the two. It was typed on the same typewriter over an extended period, as review of the quality of the type face under the magnifying glass shows how the letters have deteriorated with use over time. It also contains amendments by another party, which have been entered by hand."

"Was it not Carr himself who put in the manual changes?" I interjected.

"If you look, the person who pulls the paper out of the typewriter and hence is typing the document does so with the left hand, as some of the pages show a faint thumb mark at the top on the left-hand side. The person who makes the manual amendments does so writing with the right hand."

"You can tell that from their handwriting?"

"Not so much from that as from the fact that the person writing by hand does so while having a sandwich in his left hand. The breadcrumbs from the sandwich have fallen onto the pages on the left side of the paper and are sometimes over-written by the manual corrections but they are never over-typed. That was what I was using my magnifying glass and microscope for, as the broad pattern of the scatter is very particular. This suggests that the other person is a close acquaintance of Carr as he is showing him his work. Yet he is one who does not take the task very formally as he would hardly be eating and reading at the same time if that were the case."

“Is it not possible that Miss Brusher, who is a professional typist, typed the document and that Carr made the manual amendments?”

“My dear Watson, that explanation had of course occurred to me, but the typing is of too poor a quality to be by a professional typist. Look at the errors and corrections made by the typist of this document. Such errors would not occur to a professional, so I believe there is a second person with whom Carr is working. The second person advises Carr on his output after each section of the typescript is completed. He probably does it over lunch which explains the dropping of food onto the paper. Carr himself is typing this while he is at work as the paper is of the standard mass-produced quality used in businesses and Miss Brusher makes no mention of Carr typing at the lodgings. This suggests Carr and the other party work in close proximity to each other.”

“You seem more interested in the second party than you are in Carr himself or Miss Brusher.”

“Miss Brusher seems to me to be purely an occasional sounding board for Carr and is only of interest to us for having brought this case to our attention. Beyond his untidy eating habits, and that it is likely he meets Carr close to his workplace, I can tell little about the second party. Carr obviously trusts him as otherwise he would not be showing him his work. The second party makes frequent changes to Carr’s work with a pencil with high graphite content, one that is sharpened only very irregularly with a blunt pocket-knife, but these hardly amount to details that will readily enable us to identify him. The changes are stylistic rather than substantive and replace vague terms with more specific ones. For example, in the first sentence, the word "arrested" replaces the original typed word "caught" and this suggests a high level of education in the second party. I think that Carr regards him as a figure of authority as he has not sought to reverse any of the changes the second party has made."

"And Carr?"

"I have already indicated that he is an indifferent typist. I would also observe that in his narrative he describes himself as Company Secretary at a bank, which suggests that Miss Brusher's fellow lodger occupies a senior position and enjoys a high income." He tailed off and gazed into the yonder.

"So you think that what Carr writes about himself in the narrative actually corresponds to his real situation?" I broke in.

"Miss Brusher says that Carr is a fellow lodger of hers, that he works at a bank and that he presses his life story on her. All these details conform to this typescript which has a strange narrative style as, although it is in the third person, it is told entirely from the point of view of Carr. In the section Miss Brusher read out, he is arrested but not charged and, in later sections, he goes to committal proceedings in a particularly down-at-heel part of town. The proceedings as described are farcical. He complains about his treatment at his arrest and says the officials who arrested him have stolen his possessions, but these accusations seem to have no impact on the officials of the court who are processing his case. One is constantly left to wonder whether this is a description of actual events or something more fantastical. These are uncharted waters indeed ..." Holmes's speech lacked its normal incisiveness as he sank again into thought.

"And what are to be your next steps?"

"I shall continue to introspect," said Holmes with a yawn and, pulling his violin onto his knee, drew the bow languidly across the strings to make an inchoate sound I would not categorise as music.

"I need to decide," he continued. "Is anything criminal or untoward happening? And if so, is this something I should investigate myself, or should I turn it over to the authorities and, given the nature of the text, to which authorities? The results of my introspections may of course alternatively lead me to the conclusion that Carr is something of a bore who likes reading his rather dull, largely fictional works out to his fellow lodger and others who have little choice but to listen to them. My instinct at present, however, is against what would be a rather tame resolution to the events, even though it does explain all of them. In my view, there is a case for us to investigate, although what direction it will take us in, I would be unwilling to speculate."

My pulse quickened with excitement at Holmes's comment.

"Is there anything I can do to help you in our investigation?"

"Be prepared, dear boy, be prepared. Your main limitation and your main strength are that you are a man of action rather than of thought. I need to focus my thoughts and I shall be surprised indeed if there is not some need for action in the next few days."

When I came down the next morning I was unsurprised to find Holmes slumped in the same position as I had left him, and the air in the sitting room laden with the bitter reek of tobacco, mingled with the heavy smell of strong coffee.

"As you see, Watson, I have been up all night and, though a fixture here, I have at least found my way into Joseph Carr's world."

"And have you come to any conclusions?" I asked.

"Only negative ones so far. I have reviewed my files and the recent press. There is no legal action official or private being taken against Carr and no criminal offence of which he is a suspect."

"And what about the narrative?"

"I have read to the end of what Miss Brusher has brought us. The document is incomplete inasmuch as it does not come to a conclusion, but each chapter is essentially complete in its own right, which leads me to think that there will be further chapters to come."

"Have you then formed a view on whether it is a work of fiction or a work of record?"

"Carr is undoubtedly writing factual information when he describes himself as working at a bank. He is the Company Secretary of C&S Bank, which is headquartered at Aldersgate. I was able to track this down by reference to some of the depositions the bank has been making on its non-cash assets to the Government. Among the other events he mentions in this work, he talks of going to a courthouse in Hackney even though the court appears to be of a somewhat informal nature. I know of no legal buildings in the area that Carr describes."

"So do you propose to go down to Hackney to see whether this courthouse really exists?"

"Carr discloses a road name where the courthouse is, but no house number for where the courthouse might be. Indeed, when he set off to Hackney, he did not have this vital detail at all. He ended up having to try to gain access to the houses by the device of asking people if they knew of a Captain Spear, a name he made up based on the name of another lodger in the room adjoining his. Once inside, he used the pretext of asking after Spear to look around within the building for a courtroom."

"So are you going there this morning?"

"My dear Watson, I have already delayed my chemical research by a day to investigate what may prove to be nothing more than a somewhat rambling work of fiction. Accordingly, I propose that you should go down to Hackney this morning to see whether there is anything in Carr's narrative we can substantiate."

I was crestfallen to be sent on a task Holmes so obviously thought may well be a fool's errand, especially as his preferred activity was chemical analysis, which frequently rendered our sitting room all but uninhabitable yet which seemed to produce very few results. However, I had no activities of my own on hand, so I agreed.

Carr's typescript had disclosed that the courthouse was in Caesar Street. When I got there, it turned out to be a long road with high residential blocks on both sides. There were children playing a variety of games on the street and assorted residents performing chores like ironing, cleaning boots and sharpening knives either in their doorways or at the window of rooms facing out onto the street. The air was foggy and fetid.

I examined each rather dowdy block carefully for an indication of one which might contain the courtroom, but none gave any sign that it might do so. In the end, I decided I would have to follow Carr's own device for gaining access to the tenements and started to stop passers-by to ask them if they knew of a Captain Spear.

Verily the English are a helpful race. Within a few minutes I had learnt details about the inhabitants of the street, some of whom had been to sea, and some of whom had a name which if not Spear had at least a connection with combat – Archer, Gunn, Bowyer, Fletcher – and I had been shown into any number of buildings, none of which contained anyone called Captain Spear and were entirely devoid of any courtroom.

Carr's expedient had expedited nothing and I was back on the street on the point of heading back to the station when an elderly lady in slippers opened the door to yet another tenement house, shuffled down the stairs at the front of the building and asked: "Are you another gentleman who said he was looking for Captain Spear?"

"Yes," I replied half-truthfully. "Do you know where I might find him?"

"What you are seeking is through here," she said and headed back up the stairs.

I followed her up and at the top of the stairs, I could look past her through the door into an interior quite different to the interiors of the other buildings I had seen. It was a large, darkened room with a raised platform and a droning of voices apparently transacting some sort of official business.

I was about to go in when the lady turned to me and blocked my way, saying: "This was not meant for you."

"Then why did you come down the stairs to help me?" I asked.

"I heard you were asking for Captain Spear, sir, like the other gentleman. I probably took more on myself than I should have done by coming down the stairs and talking to you. I really don't know much about this at all," she said in a low voice, and looked around surreptitiously as though to ensure we could not be overheard. "But I knew what it was you were looking for and I thought I should at least show you where you might be able to find it. In any case, Captain Spear is not here and this door was meant to admit the gentleman who was first looking for him only."

With this the door closed abruptly in my face and no amount of calling out or knocking prevailed upon her to open it. I looked for windows but this was the one building on the street with no windows at ground level. I looked around. The street was now empty of people and the sun had come out. I could see no purpose in staying any longer and was relieved to head back to Baker Street.

Holmes's face grew longer and longer as I recounted my experience. Finally he said: "Well in all the tasks I have set you, I can think of none where the harvest of information you returned with has been so scant."

"That may be because of the difficulty of the task set," I retorted.

"Hardly so, Watson, hardly so. Why did you not ask for a courthouse rather than trying to gain access to the houses in the same ineffectual way as Carr? Why did you not try and find a landlord who might have been able to give you an overview of the street and its inhabitants? Why, you seem not even to have noted the number of the house where you looked into the large room!"

"Maybe you would have done no better," I responded. "And I did note the house number, which is more than Carr did," I added sourly, for I was hurt by his lack of empathy on the performance of a task which was far from straightforward. "It was eighty-four."

"I think any fair observer would conclude that I have done considerably better than you. While you were hunting for Captain Spear in Hackney, I searched the land registry and hunted down the identity of the landlord from those parts. Caesar Street is a development thrown up twenty years ago to provide accommodation for employees of the local blacking factory. The factory owner is the landlord and he has the sort of arbitrary ideas about how other people should live which you can impose on them when you are both their employer and landlord. The tenancy management is farmed out to the company whose representative I spoke to at his office in Regent Street this morning. All the blocks are made out of the same grey brick and with the same intention of squeezing as many poor people into the smallest amount of space possible. Anyone who works at the factory is obliged to live in the blocks around Caesar Street, the development is dry, the owner insists that the inhabitants are not allowed to hang washing up outside and that the streets are clear of people between twelve and one each day."

"But what relevance does that have to Miss Brusher's story?" I asked, as I was still sore at Holmes's high-handedness.

"The reason why I asked about the house numbers is that in one house there was a dispute with the builders during its construction and, in protest, the builders bricked up the windows on the ground floor and refused to build the non-load-bearing partition walls. The dispute was resolved and eventually the bricked-up space was used for hanging washing, whereas normally such activity is carried out in the attics. In this case, the attic area was turned into dwellings. The house number is eighty-four, so I have succeeded in finding the location of the room to which Carr was admitted although I have barely had to stir from our quarters." Holmes looked up at me from his chair and for all my frustration with my own investigations I had to own that he had found out far more than I had.

"So was my visit to Hackney a complete waste of time?" I asked in the hope of eliciting at least some small word of praise.

"Not at all, Watson, not at all," soothed my friend and leaned back in his chair. "You have confirmed what I have established by talking directly to the property manager – namely that there is a windowless room at the ground level of a block at eighty-four Caesar Street and that Carr or some man in his pay has been in Caesar Street on the pretext of looking for a Captain Spear. We can therefore rule out the theory that what Miss Brusher has told us is a complete fiction either on her part or on Carr's. You have further confirmed the presence of some sort of large room where what appears to be official business is being transacted."

I was about to make a mildly self-congratulatory comment that I had at least confirmed something even without establishing anything new when Holmes added: "It is, however, fair to say that your contribution to our investigation so far says more about your skill for accurate reporting than it does for any proper understanding of detective work."

He sat silently in his armchair and puffed indigo smoke rings at the ceiling. They hovered around the lamp-shade and dissipated. I felt the silence awkward and asked "So you say that Carr or someone in his pay has been down there? Are you suggesting it may not have been Carr who went down there since that is what he is described in Miss Brusher's text as doing?"

"Carr is clearly a troubled individual. It is not impossible that he set the whole thing up himself: gaining access to number eighty-four Caesar Street, paying people to impersonate a court and, having followed Miss Brusher here, organising for a bunch of loafers to impersonate a court for anyone following up on his narrative. He may even have arranged for someone else to go down there on his behalf rather than going down himself. Beyond some form of perverse self-gratification, however, I do not see what end that would serve and I am therefore inclined to dismiss the theory that this is all an elaborate invention on the part of Carr's, without ruling it out altogether. As you will realise, Watson, we are in the process of razoring away the impossible to leave what must be true. If we dismiss the theory that the whole thing is an elaborate fantasy on the part of Carr, in my view, there are only two possibilities left."

I waited for Holmes to set out the two possibilities, but instead he adopted an even more languorous expression and puffed more smoke rings at the ceiling. Finally I ventured an "And?"

"And I must carry out more investigations of my own," he replied calmly and leant further back in his armchair with a glazed look in his eyes.

All further efforts to draw Holmes into dialogue were unavailing and in the end I went to spend the rest of the day at the billiard table in my club. When I returned, Holmes had gone, though the acrid smell of tobacco hanging in the air assured me that he had not been gone long and that he had spent the time till his departure in a smoking frenzy.

I saw little of Holmes over the next few days. When he was in Baker Street, he was distracted far beyond conversation and it was clear that it was the case of Joseph Carr to which he was giving his full attention as his mail remained unopened and calls from visitors were rebuffed with an abruptness that he showed only when dedicating himself fully to a particularly consuming task. The one person to whom he did give an audience was Miss Brusher, who called on two separate occasions when Holmes chanced to be at our lodgings. Completely at variance to his pattern of behaviour since our earliest cases together, as soon as she appeared carrying additional bundles of typescript, Holmes asked me to vacate our sitting room so that he could talk to Miss Brusher unaccompanied, which he proceeded to do at considerable length.

I could see Miss Brusher was also startled by this approach, but, as she robustly commented, she was used to Mr Carr coming to see her without anyone else present and she was a lady who could look after herself.

It was a full week after my trip to Hackney before Holmes said anything more than a brusque word to me.

One evening when he had been back for two hours and had sat in silent contemplation, not uttering a word while still dressed in a boiler suit smelling faintly of chlorine, he suddenly started to speak:

"It's like this, Watson: In his writings, Carr gets to his job at the bank early, stays there till late and either then goes home or goes looking for help from a variety of sources on the case for which he is under arrest. I decided I needed to track Carr for as much of the day as I could, so I posed as a loafer outside twelve Prague Square for when he was at his home and then joined one of the gangs that clean the various banks in the evenings in order to be inside the bank when he was there late. One of the things I had to assess was the extent to which his writings, in which he uses the third person to describe what he does, correspond to what is in fact happening in his own life. By sitting as a loafer under his window at his home and working as a cleaner at the bank in the evenings, I am able to follow what he is doing for several hours a day, though not all the time. I have a blank period during his working day when I am unable to get into the office part of the bank, a blank when he is at home inside and a blank each time he goes into a private property to consult about his case."

"I can understand you operating as a loafer, but how did you get to work as a cleaner in a bank? Surely an organisation such as a bank would readily be able to establish that you were an imposter."

"My dear Watson, you will remember from the adventure of ours that you were kind enough to chronicle as 'The Stockbroker's Clerk' that the financial institution Mawson and Williams was prepared to offer an applicant a permanent and responsible job without so much as meeting him. Can you imagine how much easier it is to infiltrate a bank when you work in a lowly position for a contractor? The bank takes no pains at all to check the bona fides of those working for its contractor and the contractor hardly more so. I have adopted a Moravian name, Vincenc Kramar, and I had to give the team master a verbal undertaking that my presence in the country was legal. After that there were no further background checks and I was free to move from bank to bank with access to all the private offices of the most senior officers. My team is a friendly, honest, hard-working crew from all corners of the earth, though I would not advocate looking too closely at their legal right to reside in the country."

"So what are your conclusions?"

"Where I am in a position to validate his writings, they confirm to the reality of his life."

"Does that mean that you believe he is the subject of a major persecution?"

"I have no choice but to do so. Everything I observe him do appears in his writings. Accordingly, I cannot believe that his writings referring to the parts of his life I cannot see are not retelling his actual experiences, *outré* though some of them are. Therefore, I have to conclude that he is subject to a persecution from authorities that are ubiquitous, well-resourced and yet unofficial, as all my research about Carr reveals there is no official interest in him at all. Accepting that what Carr is writing is what he is experiencing also puts me into the position of observing him and then shortly afterwards reading what I have seen in the writings Miss Brusher brings around. So I watch Carr go where I cannot follow him and then read in the text from Miss Brusher that he went where I saw him go and what happened when he was out of my sight. His writings about himself, if I may say so, are a good deal less embellished than what my own chronicler writes about me or indeed about himself."

"So what is happening to Carr now?" I asked, ignoring Holmes's barb.

"He constantly tries to press his documents on Miss Brusher, but I know that not just from the text but also from what Miss Brusher tells me. And, what I can also confirm from my work as a cleaner at the bank, is that he has had an encounter with a flogger."

"With a flogger?"

"You remember at his visit to the courthouse he complained about the corrupt behaviour of the officials who arrested him. I was cleaning in the mail room of the bank late one evening when Carr came past and threw open a door to a storage cupboard in the corridor outside. I went into the corridor and I was able to see from behind his shoulder into the room where two men were being flogged by a third man because they had abstracted various possessions of Carr's on his arrest. Carr made no attempt to stop the flogging and went on his way. Shortly afterwards the incident with the flogger appeared in the typescript he gave to Miss Brusher, which she then passed on to me."

"But Holmes, whatever organisation is persecuting Carr, it seems to have resources everywhere. It can set up a courtroom in a tenement block, employ people to stage the arrest of a senior figure in a bank and use its agents to punish those of its members who do not abide by its rules. What sort of organisation is of the scale to do that?"

"One playing for high stakes, in order to make the size of their organisation viable."

"So what of your two theories?"

"Either Carr is being persecuted by some arm of the state authorities so powerful and yet perverse as to be unknown to us, or this is a private persecution from an organisation that has huge resources at its disposal. As my discrete contacts with the higher circles of the government lead me to believe that this is not a state-sponsored persecution, we are forced to conclude that a major private enterprise is persecuting Carr."

"But to what end?"

"One that I intend to uncover."

With that he pulled his violin out of its case and improvised in a way that bespoke determination, for all that it was wanting in tunefulness.

Holmes had already gone when I got up the next morning and it was two days later, as I lay slouched in my armchair after dinner, contemplating going to bed, that a message came through from him asking me to get to Prague Square as soon as possible. When I got there, I found him in the company of Peter Jones, the official police agent, whose tenacity, if not whose intelligence, Holmes had always admired. Jones and Holmes were standing silently together, but as soon as I arrived and without preamble Holmes started to whisper to me as one thinking out loud.

"And I think I have found out what they are playing for. Carr is Company Secretary of the bank, but in a previous role at the bank he was on the trading floor."

"But surely a bank would never allow someone from the trading floor to move directly to working on the administrative side of the business. It means that they both place deals and then control the processing and scrutiny of the deals."

"It clearly is a breach of what is normally required for the proper running of a bank and the lack of adequate controls over what roles people play does indeed have a bearing on what I have found. In his previous role almost exactly a year ago, Carr had a counter-party who took out a large option to buy gold from him at a price of £4 2s 1d per ounce. The contract was of a size as to be beyond the authorised limit or *ultra vires* for someone in the position Carr was in at the time, but the price of gold at present is £4 1s 9d so the contract can easily be satisfied on the existing market. Furthermore, the C&S Bank has large gold reserves and so it can cover its position."

"So in spite of all your efforts, are you still searching for a real case to investigate?"

"Oh! I have two cases to investigate! The *ultra vires* transaction I have identified is a mere prelude to the main one. What would make the contract difficult to fulfil would be if the price of gold were to spike, and one of the things that would cause it to do so would be a sudden shortage of gold on the market such as might be caused if the bank's vault were robbed. I have discovered that Carr is one of the two people each of whom has half of the code that opens the bank's vault. Both codes need to be used to gain entry to the vault. I believe the other person is putting him under pressure to reveal it and so enable that other person to rob the gold."

"But if the price of gold were to rise substantially, how much would the gain be to the person who had the gold?"

"Colossal. The person holding the gold would be in possession of metal worth a gigantic sum and there would be a run on the bank as it became unable to meet its obligations, the first of its type in this country for over a hundred years."

"So how did you uncover this?"

"Carr had entered some of the details of the *ultra vires* transaction into a notebook which he keeps on his desk. The bank's security procedures were set out in a manual of operating instructions which he also conveniently left out."

"So as a cleaner you were able to penetrate the bank's inner offices and find out the details of its most material deals and its most important security measures."

"Banks often seem unable to understand the risks they are taking or the deals that they are making or to know how to protect their secrecy. Remember Mr Holder of Holder and Stevenson, who rather than locking the beryl coronet into the safe of his bank, resolved to keep it in his home overnight and told his family about it."

"So what are your steps now?"

"I was keeping you out of this one because of the devastating consequences of what is afoot. If the bank collapses, it will be unable to meet its obligations to other banks, thereby creating a run on all of them. I could not have you realising the full potential consequences of what is happening and indicating it in some way to that share speculator friend of yours, Thurston, with whom – I observed from the chalk on your thumb – you are continuing to play at billiards. I know not where the contagion caused by a run on the banks might stop. It may indeed end with people trying to withdraw money from all the banks at once. Today, however, I established that the option on the gold expires tomorrow, so the other password holder is likely to strike tonight. I therefore need the help of someone on whose support I can rely."

I had felt a little raw about Holmes leaving me out of the case and had done my best not to show it. But I was pleased that I now had an explanation for my exclusion and some confirmation that he valued my abilities.

"Would we not be better using the full resources of Scotland Yard to help us with this?"

At that moment a hansom cab drew up and two men dressed in forbidding clothing and with black top hats pulled down low stepped out. Holmes drew us behind some bushes and we watched. They rang at number twelve and were admitted. Shortly afterwards, they came out with a third person between them whom I took to be Carr.

The cab had gone and they half-accompanied, half-dragged Carr to the middle of the square and laid him out prone on the grass. A window facing onto the square was thrown open and a light shone out as they pulled him to the ground. To my horror, I saw the glint of a blade in a gloved hand. The knife was poised over Carr's throat.

Holmes, Jones and I stole up behind them with pistols drawn. Suddenly Carr cried out "Like a dog!"

We now made no attempt to conceal our onrush and the two dark-clad men looked around. Holmes fired in the air and I had them covered. The two dropped Carr and made to run, but another shot in the air from Holmes made them realise the futility of any resistance or thought of flight. They hesitatingly raised their hands.

"Good to see you again, Mr Merryweather!" said Holmes as he ripped the hat off one of the assailants. To my astonishment, I recognised one of Carr's attackers as the well-known chairman of the Board of Directors of the County and Suburban Bank whom we had previously met in the adventure I have recorded as "The Red-Headed League".

"I think I'll call you Merryweather from now on," said Holmes. "I was always puzzled how on the night of the first attempt on County and Suburban Bank you rapped on the floor of the vault with your stick on precisely the stone under which the tunnel came out. I thought at the time it might be to warn the robbers, but I had no evidence with which to substantiate it. I have now. And how good to see you here too, John Clay," he said, turning to the other man. "I don't suppose we need to ask where the money came from to procure your escape from jail."

Merryweather was too stunned by the turn of events to say anything, but Clay said "I may once again find myself in detention at your hands, Mr Holmes, but as a man with noble blood in my veins, I do insist on being called Mr Clay. Indeed, were I able to prove my belief that my birth followed a secret marriage between Lord Mason and my mother rather than just an irregular dalliance, I would expect to be called Lord Clay."

"And you, Clay, were again on the verge of a major coup. You had the option to buy gold from Carr and were about to raid the bank's vaults to empty its stocks of gold and raise the gold price to make your option much more valuable."

"Holmes," drawled Clay. "You underestimate my ambition. You seem to think I would be satisfied by the piffling profit on a bit of gold."

"And you underestimate my investigative powers," Holmes flashed back. "I also uncovered your option to sell the shares of C&S Bank at yesterday's price. The crash in the share price caused by news of the gold theft would have made your profit far greater than what it would have been on the bullion alone. Mine is a skilful business and through my craft I have organised a rushed purchase of the shares of C&S Bank. When the stock market opens in the morning, C&S Bank shares will no longer be listed and your option will have ceased to be valuable. I think you will read in your prison cell of a triumph for Northern Bank in its attempts to increase its corporate footprint in the London banking sector."

Clay's spirit left him at this revelation and he fell silent.

"And does this mean the trial I have been going through for the last year is finally over?" quavered Joseph Carr's voice from the ground. Holmes reached out with his hand and pulled Carr to his feet.

"You, Mr Carr, will have to bear the consequences of your improper conduct, first as a trader and then as Company Secretary of your bank, but I think it is fair to say you have not behaved criminally and so will not face prosecution."

"Oh sir, it is such a relief to have this matter off my shoulders! Mr Clay was blackmailing me about the deal we struck over a year ago. I had to leave comfortable quarters and the enjoyable society of my friends to come and live as a lowly tenant here in Prague Square."

"Did no one at your bank query why you were living in accommodation so obviously out of keeping with someone in your position?"

"I was Company Secretary," said Carr with an air of defiance, "and in charge of internal controls. So of course no one raised the matter with me, but I did feel that when I was arrested in the set-up Clay and Merryweather had devised that it was as if justice itself had seen the extent of my indebtedness to Clay and was going to take its course with me."

"Perhaps you will tell us the whole story, Mr Carr."

"Indeed, sir, since you seem to know most of it already. I am thirty-one and a German resident of London of many years' standing. I was originally called Josef Karr but changed my name to Joseph Carr. Until just over a year ago, I worked on the trading desk at the C&S Bank. While working there, the man you call Mr Clay took out an option of a size well over my authorised limit to buy gold. Entering into a deal which we were not supposed to, and which we did not fully understand, was not so unusual, or indeed considered particularly wrong at a bank as hungry for profits as we traders were hungry for commissions. It was, however, unusual for our counter-party to find out about it. When Mr Clay discovered my secret, he started to blackmail me. I found the only way to deal with the pressure was to write down my feelings as a narrative. Mr Merryweather is the chairman of the bank and the person to whom I report. I have always dabbled in writing and Mr Merryweather has always shown an interest in it. When I described myself as feeling as though I was caught in a trap, without telling Mr Merryweather to what I was referring, he said it was almost as if I had been arrested for an undisclosed crime, a phrase which I incorporated into my writings."

"But how did you become Company Secretary?"

"My position as trader became more and more invidious and it was with huge relief that I saw the position of Company Secretary come available and, in an attempt to escape from my problems, I applied for it. Even though I had not a shred of the relevant experience, I got the position after I made a presentation on corporate governance which was very well received by the board and by Mr Merryweather in particular. Two days later, I was arrested here in my room in Prague Square by some unknown officials and found myself subject to a process of persecution in which I feared for my life. All of this went into my narrative, which Mr Merryweather read, commented on and made amendments to. I also read it out to my neighbour, Miss Brusher."

Carr paused as though waiting for us to say something but we were all engrossed in his narrative and no one said a word as we waited for him to continue.

"As well as his interest in my writings," he finally went on, "Mr Merryweather would often talk about the secret of the password to the vault that we now shared. He had one half and I had the other and he would often make jokes about how much power we held between us and how much the secret was worth to someone who could prise it out of both of us. I was always uncomfortable about his jests, but as I reported to Mr Merryweather as Chairman of the Board of Directors, I kept quiet about it. The blackmail and the process of the trial wore me down, but I was determined to keep going as I knew Carr's option would lapse tomorrow. I would not have shouted out the password now had I not had a knife to my throat. The shame of having done so will live with me forever."

"Why did you choose 'Like a dog' as your password?"

"Sir, when you have just been promoted out of your area of expertise, are being blackmailed so that you have to stop almost all of your outgoings and are subject to what appears to be arrest and investigation when you have committed no crime, your life feels little better than that of a dog. It seemed an appropriate phrase to use when on becoming Company Secretary I was required to enter something with eight characters that was easily memorable as my half of the password to the vaults."

Jones had by this time summoned a passing constable and between them they took Clay and Merryweather into custody. Carr went with them as a witness while Homes and I returned to Baker Street. Dawn was breaking and Holmes was transformed from the morose presence of the last few weeks. He played some Bach on the violin before we sat down to an early breakfast.

"So Watson, are there points you would like me to clarify, as I assume you will chronicle 'The Trial of Joseph Carr' even if Carr produces his own version? I suspect Carr will be somewhat elusive about what his trial was about and may exaggerate some details while downplaying others. His version will probably stick to the formula of his typescript – describing his arrest, persecution and the apparent attempt on his life – while remaining silent about how close he was to bringing the banking system down. He may not even mention the motivations behind the actions of the leading players in this drama and will, like a Government investigative report, avoid finding evidence of any systemic failings in the regulation of banks. If he makes it obscure enough, it may keep professional literary critics, whose ranks I have no wish to join, in work for years as they try to deconstruct it. Your version, I am sure, will be more revealing though the Government may embargo it as it reveals its failure to regulate the city and a lack of commercial understanding at the head of a major bank. I would observe from my work as a cleaner that such failings are not confined to County and Suburban Bank."

"What did Carr mean by the authorities being attracted by guilt when he was not in fact guilty of any crime?"

"It is worth bearing in mind that in German the words for 'guilt' and 'debt' are the same. The blackmail 'debt' from which Carr was suffering when he was arrested and which resulted in him living in such straitened circumstances should have been quite sufficient to attract the attention of the authorities."

"Why does everyone from the conspiracy apart from Clay and Merryweather claim to know almost nothing about what is going on? Surely some of them must have had a deeper involvement in the plot?"

"I think that Clay and Merryweather were playing for a big prize and they wanted to keep it for themselves. They were prepared to pay the price to have top actors performing the parts required to give Carr the sense of conspiracy against him. The advantage of doing this was that the actors were highly unlikely to ask difficult questions about the parts they were playing. I suspect that the actors were instructed to make regular professions of ignorance to Carr as a defence mechanism against any probing questions. Someone playing a part does not want to depart far from a set script and saying to Carr they knew very little about the process involving him forestalled further questions."

"What do you think will happen now to the leading players in this drama?"

"The authorities can already bring Clay to trial for his previous break-in attempt at C&S Bank. They will probably be most reluctant to prosecute Merryweather for fear of drawing public attention to the inadequacies of some of the people running banks. Merryweather will almost certainly co-operate fully with the authorities and then undergo a Pauline conversion to the merits of good governance in banking. He will probably end up being given a peerage as a final flowering of his career in the city."

"And Carr?"

"In theory Carr can go back to his work as Company Secretary for the bank. With his combination of pusillanimity and greed allied to his ability to work in very different roles, it is hard to predict what he will transform himself into next."

"You seem to have an answer for everything and to have saved the world single-handedly from a banking crash. I fully intend to write an account of this adventure and your renown will spread and live on even if the truth has to wait to emerge until long after we are all gone."

Holmes stretched out silently and puffed out more smoke rings. But a smile ghosted across his face and I sensed he was pleased to think that his fame might outlive him.

Also from MX Publishing

MX Publishing is the world's largest specialist Sherlock Holmes publisher, with over a hundred titles and fifty authors creating the latest in Sherlock Holmes fiction and non-fiction.

From traditional short stories and novels to travel guides and quiz books, MX Publishing cater for all Holmes fans.

The collection includes leading titles such as *Benedict Cumberbatch In Transition* and *The Norwood Author* which won the 2011 Howlett Award (Sherlock Holmes Book of the Year).

MX Publishing also has one of the largest communities of Holmes fans on Facebook with regular contributions from dozens of authors.

www.mxpublishing.com

Also from MX Publishing

The Missing Authors Series

Sherlock Holmes and The Adventure of The Grinning Cat
Sherlock Holmes and The Nautilus Adventure
Sherlock Holmes and The Round Table Adventure

"Joseph Svec, III is brilliant in entwining two endearing and enduring classics of literature, blending the factual with the fantastical; the playful with the pensive; and the mischievous with the mysterious. We shall, all of us young and old, benefit with a cup of tea, a tranquil afternoon, and a copy of Sherlock Holmes, The Adventure of the Grinning Cat."
Amador County Holmes Hounds Sherlockian Society

www.mxpublishing.com

Also from MX Publishing

The American Literati Series

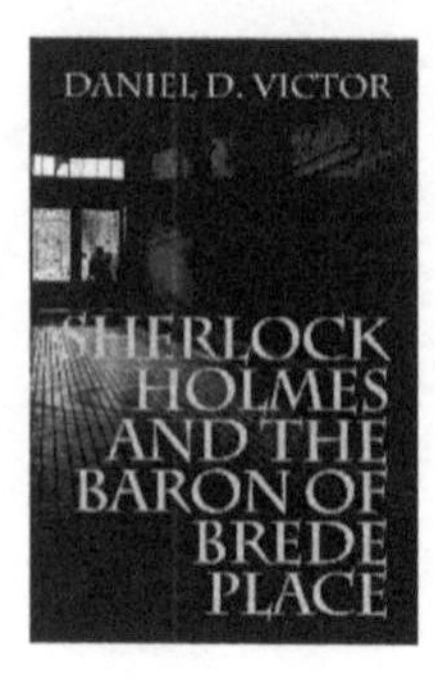

The Final Page of Baker Street
The Baron of Brede Place
Seventeen Minutes To Baker Street

"The really amazing thing about this book is the author's ability to call up the 'essence' of both the Baker Street 'digs' of Holmes and Watson as well as that of the 'mean streets' of Marlowe's Los Angeles. Although none of the action takes place in either place, Holmes and Watson share a sense of camaraderie and self-confidence in facing threats and problems that also pervades many of the later tales in the Canon. Following their conversations and banter is a return to Edwardian England and its certainties and hope for the future. This is definitely the world before The Great War."
Philip K Jones

www.mxpublishing.com

Also from MX Publishing

The Detective and The Woman Series

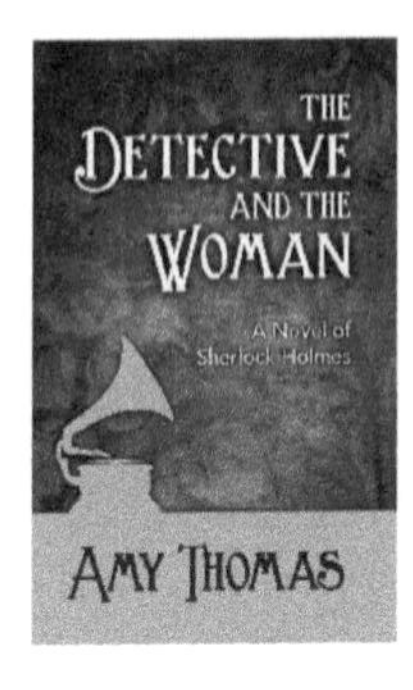

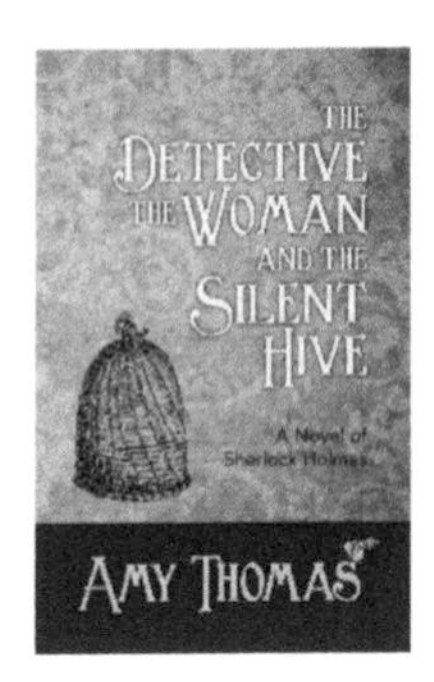

The Detective and The Woman
The Detective, The Woman and The Winking Tree
The Detective, The Woman and The Silent Hive

"The book is entertaining, puzzling and a lot of fun. I believe the author has hit on the only type of long-term relationship possible for Sherlock Holmes and Irene Adler. The details of the narrative only add force to the romantic defects we expect in both of them and their growth and development are truly marvelous to watch. This is not a love story. Instead, it is a coming-of-age tale starring two of our favorite characters."
Philip K Jones

www.mxpublishing.com